W9-CAY-651

Audrey Took A Step Closer And Faced Him,

the lamps shining a golden, halolike glow around her head.

She parted her sweet lips and her brown eyes darkened to a seductive shade. "You don't want to leave."

Slowly she reached behind and grabbed the ties of her halter top at the back of her neck. Fascinated and overwrought with desire, Luke couldn't utter a word. He couldn't tell her to stop. He couldn't tell her this was crazy. She was his mystery woman, and he'd secretly hoped to have a thrilling repeat of the night they'd shared.

"I ran away from you once, Luke. That won't happen again."

Dear Reader,

It's Luke Slade's story this time in the series The Slades of Sunset Ranch, and he's got himself in a pickle with a case of mistaken identity. Luke is a do-gooder, the man who always does the right thing, a hunky Mr. Nice Guy. (I know, I know…where can we find a guy like this in real life, right?) All his instincts tell him not to get involved with his good buddy's little sis, and he's pretty good at heeding his own advice.

But fate steps in and Luke now has a situation on his hands…and her name is Audrey Faith Thomas. Sexy T-shirts, sex texting (now I bet I got your attention) and budding true love all play a role in this tale that asks the question: what if the perfect guy for you, the one you give your heart, soul and body to, doesn't know it was you under his sheets? See what happens when Luke Slade figures out Audrey's secret in Sunset Seduction.

And while you're reading, keep an eye on Kat Grady. She's gonna drop a bombshell on returning military hero Justin Slade in the third book of The Slades of Sunset Ranch, coming this fall!

Happy reading!

Charlene Sands

Hunky heroes with heart…

CHARLENE SANDS

SUNSET SEDUCTION

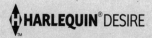
HARLEQUIN® DESIRE

If you purchased this book without a cover you should be aware that this book is stolen property. It was reported as "unsold and destroyed" to the publisher, and neither the author nor the publisher has received any payment for this "stripped book."

Recycling programs
for this product may
not exist in your area.

ISBN-13: 978-0-373-73246-3

SUNSET SEDUCTION

Copyright © 2013 by Charlene Swink

All rights reserved. Except for use in any review, the reproduction or utilization of this work in whole or in part in any form by any electronic, mechanical or other means, now known or hereafter invented, including xerography, photocopying and recording, or in any information storage or retrieval system, is forbidden without the written permission of the publisher, Harlequin Enterprises Limited, 225 Duncan Mill Road, Don Mills, Ontario M3B 3K9, Canada.

This is a work of fiction. Names, characters, places and incidents are either the product of the author's imagination or are used fictitiously, and any resemblance to actual persons, living or dead, business establishments, events or locales is entirely coincidental.

This edition published by arrangement with Harlequin Books S.A.

For questions and comments about the quality of this book, please contact us at CustomerService@Harlequin.com.

® and TM are trademarks of Harlequin Enterprises Limited or its corporate affiliates. Trademarks indicated with ® are registered in the United States Patent and Trademark Office, the Canadian Trade Marks Office and in other countries.

Printed in U.S.A.

Books by Charlene Sands

Harlequin Desire

Silhouette Desire

Harlequin Historical

CHARLENE SANDS

is a _USA TODAY_ bestselling author of thirty-five romance novels, writing sensual contemporary romances and stories of the Old West. Her books have been honored with a National Readers Choice Award, a Cataromance Reviewer's Choice Award and she's a double recipient of the Booksellers' Best Award. She belongs to the Orange County Chapter and the Los Angeles Chapter of RWA.

Charlene writes "hunky heroes with heart." She knows a little something about true romance—she married her high school sweetheart! When not writing, Charlene enjoys sunny Pacific beaches, great coffee, reading books from her favorite authors and spending time with her family. You can find her on Facebook and Twitter. Charlene loves to hear from her readers! You can write her at P.O. Box 4883, West Hills, CA 91308 or sign up for her newsletter for fun blogs and ongoing contests at www.charlenesands.com.

To Charles Griemsman for not only being my talented editor, a source of great support and a joy to work with, but for being a really amazing person, as well.

One

Usually nothing much unnerved Audrey Faith Thomas, except for the time six months ago when her big brother was bucked off Old Stormy at an Amarillo rodeo and broke his back. He was tossed eight feet in the air and landed with a solid smack to the ground. Casey's injury was severe enough to have Audrey quitting veterinary school last semester to nurse him back to health.

Audrey shuddered at the memory and thanked the Almighty that Casey was alive and well and bossy as ever. But as she sat behind the wheel of her truck driving toward her fate, the fear coursing through her veins had nothing to do with Casey's disastrous five-second ride and resulting retirement from the rodeo. This fear was much different. It scared her silly and made her doubt herself. It made her want to turn her Chevy pickup truck around and go home to Reno and forget all about showing up at Sunset Ranch unannounced.

To face Lucas Slade.

The man she'd seduced and then abandoned in the middle of the night.

Audrey swallowed hard and tried to reconcile her behavior. It wasn't working. She still couldn't believe what she'd done and after repeating her motives a thousand times in her head, nothing much had changed.

Last month, after an argument and a three-week standoff with her brother, she'd left her Reno home and ventured to his Lake Tahoe cabin to make amends. He'd been right about the boyfriend she'd just dumped, and she'd needed Casey's strong shoulder to cry on. But once she'd arrived, Casey was fast asleep on the couch and the last person she'd expected to find sleeping in the guest room, on *her bed,* was Luke Slade—the man of her fantasies, the one she'd measured every other man against. Luke was the guy she'd crushed on during her teen years while traveling the rodeo circuit with Casey—the guy who'd treated her with kindness and the same sort of brotherly love that Casey had.

Seeing him sent all rational thoughts flying out the window. This was her chance. She wouldn't let her prudish upbringing interfere with what she needed. His right arm was in a soft cast. That hadn't stopped her from edging closer.

Luke's eyelids had parted and two partially opened slits of warm blue honed in on her. "Come closer," he'd rasped in the darkened room. She'd taken that as an invitation to climb into bed with him, the consequences be damned. That night, her heart and soul, as well as her body, had been involved.

Well…she'd gotten a lot more than a shoulder to cry on, and it had been glorious and amazing and out and out wonderful. How could it not be? She'd been secretly in love with her brother's good buddy for years.

Audrey sent Jewel, the orange tabby sleeping in the travel carrier next to her, an apologetic glance. "It wasn't like he was some random guy. It was *Luke,*" she told the cat as if that explained it all. Her cat, who hadn't been much company on the drive, opened her eyes and gave her a stare before returning to cat dreamland. Audrey focused her attention back on the winding two-lane road, a shortcut through the Sierra Nevada Mountains to Sunset Ranch.

Audrey lowered the brim of her bright pink ball cap, shading her eyes from the glaring sun, and reached back to straighten out her ponytail. Coming through the mountain pass, she made the turn off the interstate and drove a little farther. As her gaze roamed the road, she recognized wisps of tall grass, purple wildflowers and white fences signifying the manicured property surrounding Sunset Lodge. The upscale dudelike resort adjacent to the ranch was another of the Slades' prosperous enterprises. Once she passed the lodge, the ranch would be half a mile down the road.

"We're almost there," she told her sleepy cat.

Audrey couldn't relax like the mellow feline beside her. Her fingers curled tightly around the steering wheel and as her doubt and fear doubled, her heart pounded hard in her chest.

She should've stayed with Luke that night. She should've been brave enough to face him in the morning. But every time those thoughts popped into her head, she had images of Casey waking up and finding her in bed with his good buddy. There was no doubt in her mind that Casey would've gone ballistic, asking no questions and taking no prisoners. She'd come to the conclusion that leaving Luke and the cabin had been the only way.

And it was a good thing her brother slept like the dead and hadn't had a clue she'd had a booty call with his best friend.

Two days later, once she'd gotten the nerve to call her brother, she'd learned the reason for Luke's visit. He'd been trampled by a horse in an awful accident. His arm had been broken along with three ribs. He'd come to Casey's Lake Tahoe cabin to recuperate.

Now, she would finally come face-to-face with Luke. She'd confront him about the night they'd shared and confess her love for him, if it came down to that. She wondered if he thought her easy, a one-night stand and a woman who didn't know her own mind. What had he thought about her abandoning him that night?

She would soon find out. She drove deeper onto Slade land and the gates came into view. Overhead, a wrought-iron emblem depicting the sun setting on the horizon marked the east entrance to Sunset Ranch. She slowed the truck to a near crawl, losing some of her nerve.

She could make a U-turn, head home and no one would be the wiser.

Behind her, a driver in a feed truck packed with hay bales laid his hand on the horn startling her out of her reverie. She took it as an omen. *Drive on. Head toward your destiny, whatever it may be.*

She did just that, and a few minutes later, holding her breath and feigning bravado, Audrey parked her truck, grabbed the cat carrier and knocked on Luke's door.

When the door opened, she faced Lucas Slade. A gasp caught in her throat and she swallowed it down with one gulp. She drank in the sight of him, and her heart stirred restlessly, like all the other times she'd been in Luke's company. She was hopeless.

Sunlight played in his dark blond hair and touched his face on a day when he hadn't shaved. Rugged, appealing and so handsome she could cry. He stood a full head taller than she did. As a young girl, she'd thought if she could catch up to his height it would put her on even footing with him on other levels. It had been a silly whim that had never materialized. Luke was tall; she stood at average height. Five years separated their ages, which had seemed like an aeon to a teenager with a crush.

A little dumbfounded, she stared at him, not wanting to blow it by blurting out the wrong thing. She held her tongue and waited for him to say something.

His brows drew together. "That you under that hat, Audrey Faith?"

Heavens, she'd forgotten about the darn hat. She nodded and lifted the brim a little.

A big smile lit his face and sparkled in his eyes. "Well, come here."

He didn't wait for her to move. He stepped forward with his arms outstretched. At that moment, all of her fears were put to rest. He was glad to see her. *Lord, have mercy.*

But when she expected to be swept into an embrace and kissed the way he'd kissed her in the cabin, he bypassed her lips completely. Instead, her face was smothered by his shoulder as he gave her a big welcoming bear hug. There was no doubt about the affection there, or in the two *brotherly* pats to her shoulders, either, before he took a step back to look at her.

"What brings you out to Sunset Ranch?" His gaze whipped over her shoulder. "Did Casey drive out with you, too?"

"Oh, uh…no. Casey isn't with me."

"Okay," he said with a nod. "Well then, come inside, out of the heat. And bring whatever pet you've rescued with you."

She'd forgotten about the tabby in the carrier she'd set down on the porch. "H-her name is Jewel. She was hit by a car two months ago and was in shock for a while. Now she gets separation anxiety if I leave her for too long."

Luke gave the cat a better look through the carrrier's mesh window. "She made the trip from Reno with you?"

Her pulse quickened as his blue-eyed gaze returned to hers. She nodded.

"Lucky cat. I bet you're giving her the royal treatment. You always were great with animals."

She stood there, bewildered by Luke's reaction. He didn't make any acknowledgment about seeing her again. Or about that night that had rocked her world. He didn't seem angry, hurt, relieved or much of *anything.* She hadn't known exactly what to expect when she got here, but his civility clearly wasn't it.

Her feet wouldn't move, and her hesitation didn't faze him. He simply lifted the handle of the cat carrier and swung it along as he walked toward the parlor.

Audrey grabbed hold of her mind, and followed behind.

"You're a sight for sore eyes, Audrey Faith," he said over his shoulder.

So was he. Her throat constricted as she recalled the dreams she'd had of him for the past four weeks. Now she was here with him in the flesh. "I like to be called Audrey now. I dropped the Faith a few years ago."

Luke chuckled, and it was deep and rich and full of raw sensuality, just like she'd remembered. Of course, back when she was a teen, she didn't know much about sensuality. She only knew that she loved the sound of his laughter. "All right, *Audrey*," he said, softlike.

Mercy. Her belly warmed from the delicious way he said her name.

Audrey gave herself a mental shake as she walked behind him into the house. She managed to keep her eyes trained *off* his perfect butt fitted into Wranglers. Instead, she concentrated on Luke's dark blond hair that reached past his collar to curl at his shoulders. The strands were much longer now. She remembered threading her fingers through those thick, healthy locks. How she yearned to do it again.

That entire night seemed like a surreal dream.

Luke set the cat carrier down on the sofa and turned to face her. "It's really good to see you, Audrey. It's been a long time."

How long was a long time? She'd seen him one month ago.

"Same here," she said. This wasn't how she'd expected this conversation to go. In her wildest imaginings, Luke would have been thrilled to see her. He would have whisked her off to his bedroom, claiming undying love and demanding that she never leave his side again. In the worst-case scenario,

Luke would've scolded her for having unprotected sex with him and then running off in the middle of the night.

But *this* conversation was just plain strange.

"I'm glad you came for a visit," Luke said, gesturing for her to take a seat.

She sat down next to the cat carrier. Luke took a seat across from her in a buttercup-colored wing chair trimmed with round bronzed studs. "You look great."

She didn't think so. When she'd dressed this morning, she'd picked the best her neglected wardrobe had to offer, plaid blouse, baggy jeans and her too-long hair tucked into a baseball cap. She'd been meaning to get a stylish cut but that obviously hadn't happened. The ball cap and casual clothes were Audrey As Usual. "Thanks, so do you. Are you feeling better?"

"I've got no complaints. My arm's good as new now." His arm had been encumbered with a cast when they made love, but that hadn't stopped him from making her die a thousand pleasant deaths that night.

"That's…good."

"What've you been up to?" he asked, being polite.

"I, uh… *Luke?*" She hated to sound desperate, but Luke was avoiding the whole I-jumped-your-bones-in-the-middle-of-the-night subject.

His eyes softened and his voice registered sympathy. "What's up, honey? You have another fight with Casey? Is he still being a bear?"

She leaned back against the seat cushion, rattled. Was he being deliberately obtuse? Surely he had to know why she'd come this distance to visit him.

Luke was a wealthy horse breeder now. Along with his brothers, he owned the biggest ranch in three counties. He had a lot on his mind, and it humbled her to think he remembered her troubles with Casey. It had been years since Audrey had complained to Luke about her brother's overprotective, overbearing nature. She would confide in Luke, because he was the only one who'd really listened to her and treated her as an equal rather than a silly girl with years of growing up to do.

"We still argue," she said, "but it's different now."

"How so?" He seemed genuinely interested.

"He can't ground me anymore, so I really let him have it."

Luke laughed again. "I bet you do."

Audrey forced a smile. She didn't get any of this. Luke acted as if they hadn't been intimate, hadn't steamed up the sheets on that guest-room bed. Was making love to a woman such an everyday occurrence to him that Luke thought nothing of it? Just casual sex with a onetime friend? "Casey knows I'm a big girl now. He doesn't lord over me like he used to."

She wanted to make it clear to Luke that Casey didn't play into the equation. What happened between the two of them wasn't any of her big brother's business.

"So he finally cut the apron strings?"

"He's getting there. It's better than it was."

Luke nodded, and they stared at each other. "Can I get you something cold to drink?"

"No…I'm just fine."

"Okay." He nodded once again and then she caught him glancing at his watch.

"Am I keeping you from something?"

"Nope," he said, sitting up straighter in his seat, giving her his full attention. Luke was the best fibber on the planet. On the rodeo circuit, he used to tell white lies all the time to make people feel better.

Yes, Mrs. Jenkins, your strawberry-rhubarb pie is the best in the county.

Jonathan, you just need another year practicing with that fiddle before you make it to the Grand Ole Opry.

No, Audrey Faith, you're not keeping me from anything important.

Audrey knew it was now or never. She had to speak with

Luke about that night. She couldn't leave things the way they were without clearing the air.

"I actually do have a reason for being here, Luke," she said softly. "I think you know why, but if you're going to make me say it…"

Luke's forehead wrinkled as he gave it some thought. Then it hit him. "Ah…Audrey." He raised his hand to stop her. "Say no more. I should've guessed the second I saw you standing on the doorstep."

Relieved, Audrey let her stiff shoulders relax. Finally, they would get things out in the open.

"You heard about the wrangler job at the ranch," he said. "Casey must've told you I was shorthanded. Come to think about it, there's no one better to help me settle down my pain-in-the-ass, hardheaded stallion. I should have thought of hiring you myself, but we haven't talked in years, so it didn't cross my mind. The truth is, I need to get Tribute in line. He's a big challenge. Casey tells me you're not going back to vet school until the fall?"

Blood drained from her face and a shudder of dread coursed through her body. Her devastation would be visible any second now. She couldn't let that happen.

Get a grip, Audrey. Hang on.

She was finally getting the picture. It was murky at best. "I, uh…y-yes, that's my plan," she managed.

She wished she'd chickened out instead of coming here. She could have done a quick one-eighty on the highway and headed straight back to Reno. Because the murkiness was clearing and the image left underneath was nightmarishly ugly.

We haven't talked in years.

She could take that literally. Technically, they hadn't talked…much. They'd moaned and groaned their way through that night. But she'd be an even bigger fool than she was now if she thought that's what Luke had meant.

The Luke she'd known in the past wouldn't have skirted an issue this big. He would have been up front and honest. He would have probably apologized and felt guilty as hell for making love to his best friend's little sister. There was only one conclusion that Audrey could draw. There was only one reason any of this made sense.

Luke doesn't know he made love to me.

That incredible night of passion they'd shared was one-sided.

He wasn't being obtuse. He was clueless.

If someone plunged a dagger in her heart, the pain couldn't have been any greater.

"What do you say, honey?" The timbre of his deep voice broke through her anguish.

"Want to spend what's left of the summer with me on Sunset Ranch?"

"They're just formalities, Audrey, but we've got to do them," Luke said as he handed her an application for the job on Sunset Ranch.

She sat in the Slade family office located at one end of the sprawling one-story ranch house. Luke had taken a seat at his desk across from her. She felt his eyes on her as she began filling out the personal information on the form. Robotically, she went about accepting the job as wrangler on the Slades' very lucrative horse farm, her mind on automatic pilot as she tied herself to working with Lucas Slade for the next two months.

Audrey wasn't into science fiction, but she could surely relate to anyone who believed in alternate universes. This sci-fi version of her life had her living under Luke's roof and working beside him every day, filling her summer days with something more than meaningless temp jobs back home until she could restart her veterinary education. This universe wasn't ideal, but it was a far cry better than anything reality had had to offer.

Audrey completed the application. As she leaned forward to hand Luke the form, the fresh lime scent of his cologne brought memories of kissing his throat and shoulders and chest. It was the same scent that had lingered on her long after she'd fled her brother's cabin.

Luke glanced at the application for less than five seconds, before smiling and standing. "You're hired. Let me show you to your room."

And within minutes, Audrey stood alone in her new bedroom, slightly dazed by what had occurred during the past thirty minutes.

She'd discovered she'd made love to a man who didn't remember doing the deed.

He'd offered her a dream job.

And insisted she live in a guest bedroom less than twenty feet from his own room.

Audrey glanced at Jewel, who was stretched out lengthwise on the bedspread, a tiger-striped bundle of fur against black-and-bright-yellow flowers. The beautiful space was bigger than any room she'd ever called her own. And yet, as she glanced around the opulent surroundings, she questioned her decision to take the job, muttering, "What have I done?"

Audrey didn't have to wonder for very long. Immediate clarity punched her in the gut. She'd done what she had to do. No way could she have walked out the door, never to see Luke again. The second she'd laid eyes on him today that possibility wasn't an option. She finally came out of her thirty-minute fog and realized she was where she needed to be. She had been given another chance with Luke.

Yes, her heart was broken that Luke had forgotten their night together because her memories of him were profound, unforgettable. Her responses to his heady kisses severed all ties she had to good-girl status. She'd moved on him, mindful of his encumbered arm, in wild, wicked ways that had astonished her afterward. But while in the moment, she'd let go and ridden his tight, hard, muscled body until he was ready to guide her home.

I'll never forget.

A satisfied purr escaped her throat. The cat's head came up.

She stifled a chuckle and walked over to the bed. "Go back to sleep, Jewel," she whispered, taking a seat and stroking the cat's soft underbelly until her eyes drifted closed again.

Oh, to trade places with the cat right now. To have no worries and no heartache and sleep away the day…what could be better?

Audrey allowed herself a few minutes of self-pity and then tried to look on the bright side of things. At least Luke had faith in her. That was a plus. He'd hired her for a job that wasn't easily won on the highly respected ranch, not because of his friendship with Casey, but because she had a way with animals. He trusted her abilities and needed her help with the dang horse that had trampled him and sent him to the hospital.

She would look upon Trib as a challenge that she could conquer.

Getting Luke to see her as anything other than his buddy's baby sister would involve a heck of a lot more work.

"I know we'll be good together," Luke had said, right before he'd walked out of the guest room.

Audrey sighed.

If he only knew how true that statement was.

As soon as Luke showed Audrey to her room, he went back into the office to give her application another glance. Audrey Faith Thomas, half sister to Casey—though nobody much mentioned the *half* part anymore—had had a rough upbringing. She'd lost her parents early on, and Casey had raised her. She'd been the tagalong little sis on the rodeo circuit. Luke thought that Audrey had gotten a raw deal in life. Casey had been overly strict with her. Luke figured her brother was overcompensating, being mother and father to her. Casey had tried hard, but a lot of the time, he didn't know what the hell he was doing when it came to his little sister.

Audrey compensated, too. She took to the animals and the animals loved her in return. They were a good match. Audrey had a special fondness for the rodeo horses. There wasn't a one that didn't temper its wild mood when Audrey walked up.

According to her application, after college, she'd worked for a veterinarian clinic in Reno for a couple of years before deciding to apply to equine vet school. Luke also noted all the charity and volunteer work Audrey had done through the years. She had listed animal shelters and horse rescues, and was part of the Freedom for Wild Horses organization.

Luke picked up the phone and punched in Casey's number. "Hey," he said when his friend answered.

"Hey."

Luke owed his friend a favor for letting him crash at his Tahoe cabin last month. Being with his buddy helped his recuperation move along more quickly. Well, at least it'd been less mentally painful. Luke thought he'd go stir-crazy, not being able to do a dang thing with his arm in a cast and three cracked ribs making it hard for him to breathe. Up at the cabin, it was okay to do nothing but while away the time. Casey made it easy and they'd had a few laughs.

But he would have hired Audrey even if he didn't owe Casey a favor. She was qualified and a hard worker. Audrey was true blue and a nice kid.

"I've got your little sis here. She's working for me now."

There was silence on the other end. And finally "She didn't tell me that."

Uh-oh. Luke didn't like getting in between the two of them. "Yeah, well, it just happened. You must've mentioned that I was shorthanded on the ranch. Anyway, she showed up looking for work, and I hired her as a wrangler for a few months."

"Hell, Luke. I don't recall mentioning any such thing to her. I must be getting old and forgetful."

Luke laughed. Casey was only thirty-three. "Hell, yeah, you are. You see any problem with her working here?" Not that Luke was asking permission. Audrey was twenty-four and making her own decisions now. He'd called Casey for an entirely different reason.

Casey hesitated. "Not at all, buddy. It's just that she's been acting a little weird lately. You know, sort of wanting to be by herself and all. I thought she'd come up to the cabin to spend the summer with me. She had this loser boyfriend in Reno and she finally dumped him. The jerk was cheating on her. My little sis really took it hard. I don't think she's over it yet. It was all I could do to restrain myself from knocking his stupid self from here to Sunday. Jackass."

"Jackass is right."

"Damn straight."

"Well, she's here now," Luke said. "She's going to be staying at the main house. You don't need to worry. I'll look out for her."

"Like you always do. I appreciate it, Luke. And I'll count on you to make sure none of those ranch hands break her heart."

"Hell, she'll be breaking theirs."

Casey chuckled. "That's all right, then."

"Yeah, I hear you. Don't worry about Audrey. And you come up anytime you want to visit. Stay at the ranch."

"What, and leave my cabin? I got me a keg of beer, my barbecue grill and gorgeous women to stare at by the lake all day long."

Luke's mind flashed an image of one gorgeous woman in particular—a blonde with long, slender legs and a dazzler of a smile—who had crashed the lakeshore party Casey had thrown on Luke's last night at the cabin. She'd shown up at his farewell barbecue and had caught his eye the second she'd walked over to join the festivities. She'd been with a small group of people and Luke never did get the woman's name amid the fifty or so partygoers that Casey had invited. She'd come late and left early, but not before giving Luke half a dozen suggestive looks. He'd been ready to approach her, but had gotten sidetracked by someone interested in hearing about his rodeo days.

"You ever find out who that blonde was?" Luke had good reason to ask.

"You mean the stunner?" Casey asked. "I was drunk, but not too drunk to see how fine she was."

"So you know who I'm talking about."

"I found out her name is Desiree."

"And?"

"She's an acquaintance of one of my neighbors. She lives on the East Coast somewhere. She's gone. That's all I know, man. You missed your chance."

Luke wasn't going to divulge what had happened with the blonde to Casey. Luke kept his private life private. But since he'd been accepting his friend's hospitality and living at his cabin for a few weeks, a surge of guilt washed over him for not being completely truthful with Casey. Though having a one-night stand with a stranger, no matter how beautiful, wasn't exactly something to brag about. Not in this day and age. He wasn't eighteen anymore. He was old enough to know better. His only excuse was that he'd been in a haze. Drugged up on pain meds.

Vague memories of that night continually plagued him.

At least now he knew who the mysterious woman was. She'd taken the reins that night, which suited him fine since his injuries prohibited much mobility, and his mind was pretty fogged up. At times he'd thought he'd dreamed the whole thing except that he did remember small details, like her fresh-flower scent, her long flowing blond hair caressing his cheek and his completely sated body and good mood when he'd woken up that morning.

"Well, the mystery is solved," Luke said, thinking it for the best that she lived so far away. One-night stands weren't his thing but neither were complicated affairs. Luke had yet to meet a woman who held his interest for too long. Most of his relationships lasted less than six months before one of them realized that something was missing. Luke never felt the need to explore what that something was. If it wasn't right there, pounding in his heart and making him silly crazy, what was the point of forcing it? He'd done that once with a girl in high school, trying hard to hang on, to convince her it was working, and in the end, he'd been the one who'd gotten his heart shattered.

Usually when he entered into a relationship with a woman, if the flow wasn't smooth and easy from the get-go, Luke was the first one to bail.

"Too bad, though," Casey said. "She was smokin' hot."

Yep, she was. There was no arguing that point. From what he could remember, she'd been a hellcat in bed. But he let the comment drop and turned the conversation to a new venture Casey was thinking about going into since he'd been forced into retirement with his back injury.

After a few minutes, Casey ended the phone call with a last parting remark. "Thanks for helping my little sis out, Luke. You're her second brother. I know you'll look out for her."

"You got my promise on that, Case. I won't let you down."

Two

Audrey grabbed her canvas overnight tote from her truck. She didn't know what to expect when she arrived here without an invitation—certainly not to be hired on Sunset Ranch—but she'd brought a few essentials and a change of clothes with her, just in case things worked out with Luke. A girl could be optimistic, couldn't she? At the very least, she assumed that Luke would've remembered making love to her. It was a given, or so she'd thought. There had been *two* people on that bed, sighing and groaning with pleasure, for the better part of an hour.

Now that she was staying on the ranch *as an employee* for a couple of months, she'd have to do some shopping in town to get a few more changes of clothes. She'd placed a call to Susanna Hart half an hour ago. Her next-door neighbor and good friend back in Reno had the key to her house—technically, Casey's house—where she'd grown up, at least when she wasn't traveling from town to town on the rodeo circuit. Casey hadn't allowed her to stay home by herself much when

she was in high school. Susanna's mother would watch out
for her when she had a big test at school or something; otherwise, she tagged along with her brother.

Her high school experience had been grim, and she'd struggled to get good grades and keep up with events that were
important to her. Senior year had been hard, and though she'd
dreamed of Luke taking her to the prom, she'd settled on
going with a nice boy who'd also been somewhat of an out-
cast.

Susanna had offered to pack up her clothes, her laptop, a
few photos and Jewel's favorite cat bowl and send them on.
Audrey hadn't gone into detail about her situation other than
to tell her friend that she'd be working on Sunset Ranch with
the horses for the summer.

As she gazed at Jewel snoring lightly on the bed, Audrey
wished she could be as oblivious to the world around her as
her feline buddy. The bed looked inviting, and she wasn't supposed to officially start her job until tomorrow. But it was the
middle of the day and she wasn't much of a napper.

She walked into the bathroom to splash water on her face
and then gasped when she looked in the mirror. She gave the
image staring back at her a frown. She looked like hell. Her
eyes were rimmed with red from lack of sleep last night and
her hair, which was badly in need of a trim, was sticking out
in three places from under the hat. "Goodness, Audrey, you
look a sight."

She worked on her appearance in haste.

Right now, Audrey longed to meet the horses. As she'd
driven up, she'd seen the ranch corrals and the dozen or so
horses, standing under giant oaks that provided shade from
the other side of the fences.

Sunset Lodge had its own stable of horses, Luke had explained, that were primarily used for the lodge's guests. They
were sweet, gentle-natured animals that would provide trail
rides and hayrides to entertain visitors. But the barns on the

real working ranch housed some of the finest stallions, mares and geldings in the western half of the United States.

Casey had always bragged about the Slades's horses until Audrey's ears had burned. Her brother hadn't a clue that hearing about anything regarding Luke gave her a warm, fuzzy feeling in the pit of her stomach. Memories of him, and the fact that Luke had never married, had her daydreaming of him more times than she'd like to admit. It had sabotaged her feelings for most other men. At least until her recent boyfriend. She'd taken a chance with Toby and had really begun to like him, despite his flaws, until the day she'd learned he'd been a cheat with more than one woman.

That had been a hard pill to swallow.

And what upset her most wasn't so much that she was out a boyfriend, but that she hadn't really cared that much. Sure, she'd been hurt by his betrayal and humiliated that she'd been made a fool, but losing Toby wasn't so great a loss. What shattered her was an impending fear that she'd never settle for any man but Luke.

And clearly, he was an impossible dream.

So when the opportunity had presented itself, Audrey grabbed the brass ring. Then fool that she was, she'd lost her nerve and had run out on Luke.

"Idiot," she said, plopping her ball cap on her hopeless hair and striding out the door.

A few minutes later, she stood by the ranch's corral fence close to the trunk of a tree where three horses huddled under the umbrella of shade. One of the horses looked over. He was a beauty, a bay gelding that stood fifteen hands high, his legs marked with white socks.

She softened her tone, "Come here, boy."

The horse wandered over and Audrey put her hand over the corral fence, letting the horse sniff her scent and look into her eyes. "You're a pretty one."

The horse snorted quietly and when she was sure he felt

comfortable with her, she laid her hand on his coat and stroked his withers.

"You and I are going to be friends. Yes, we are."

Another horse wandered over and before long, all three horses were nudging each other to get some attention.

She smiled, realizing she hadn't felt this good in days.

Horses had always been her salvation.

A dog scurried by, barking at the horses for no apparent reason as he ran the perimeter of the corral. Audrey could tell it was a game between the animals. The horses paid little mind to the black-and-white Border collie.

Soon, a small boy appeared, running at full speed after the dog, his little legs making long strides. He came to a screeching stop when he saw her by the tree.

"Hello," she said.

"Hi." He looked at the ground.

"My name is Audrey Thomas. I'm a friend of Luke's. I'm going to be taking care of the horses. What's your dog's name?"

The dog stood twenty feet up ahead, having taken a break from his run to catch his breath.

"Oh, h-he's not my d-dog exactly. I w-watch him for Mr. S-Slade. H-his name is B-Blackie."

Audrey nodded. "Good name. I bet you have a good name, too."

The boy's mouth curled up. "It's E-Edward. No one c-calls me Eddie."

"I won't call you Eddie, either, Edward."

"Thanks." He glanced at the dog, patiently waiting to resume the game of chase. "I havta g-go. My g-grandma's waiting f-for me."

"Okay, nice to meet you, Edward."

The boy nodded and took off again.

Luke found her grinning when he walked up a minute later. "I see you met Edward and Blackie."

The sound of his voice hummed through her body. She couldn't look at him. She stared at the horses, who were still vying for her attention. "Yes. Seems like a sweet boy."

"Yeah, he's a good kid. Ten years old. His grandmother runs the kitchen at Sunset Lodge. It's a long story, but he loves living at the lodge. My brother Logan and I give him chores to do around here. Blackie's one of his *chores with bonuses.*"

"I'm getting the picture." She finally turned to him. His blue eyes devastated her. It was hard looking at his handsome face.

Get a grip, Audrey. You have to see him every day now.

His stomach growled and he laughed. "Sorry. The housekeeper's on vacation and I'm hopeless in the kitchen. I was going over to the lodge to scrounge a meal. You wanna come?"

"I, uh… No, thanks. Look at me. I'm not exactly lodge-worthy right now."

He pulled the bill of her cap down with an affectionate tug, just like he used to do way back when. "Sure you are."

"I'm not, really," she said, her eyes flashing. She looked like hell. She could hardly believe she'd walked up to Luke's door looking like this. "I need a shower and a fresh change of clothes. Besides, I don't want to leave Jewel alone too long. She needs to adjust to her new environment."

Lucky cat was probably sleeping the afternoon away.

Luke studied her face a second. "You still got cooking skills?"

"I can stir a pot when needed."

"I remember. You're a pretty darn good cook. Why don't you shower and change and meet me in the kitchen. Between the two of us, we can probably whip up something edible for lunch. I really don't want to beg a meal over at the lodge. Much rather spend my time sharing a meal with you."

It would hardly be begging, since Luke and his family owned the place. And she couldn't take to heart what he said about spending time with her. That throwaway line, while she thought it genuine, was merely Luke being Luke. He was cordial to everyone.

She should refuse. She should tell him she needed to rest, but who was she kidding? She had enough adrenaline pumping through her veins right now to run a marathon. Luke's beckoning eyes darkened to a deep ocean blue, causing her breath to catch in her throat. Unknowingly, he had powers of persuasion that quelled a woman's resolve. He was everyone's Mr. Nice Guy and he'd been her own private knight in shining armor. It was hard denying him anything—thus her taking up residence here and working for him on Sunset Ranch. "Okay. I'll meet you in the kitchen in thirty minutes."

His stomach complained again and he grinned like a little boy. "I'll be there."

Audrey turned on the faucet, adjusting the water temperature to medium-hot, and stepped inside the shower. As the pulsating spray hit her naked body, she closed her eyes to the warmth and relaxed as she washed away the dusty morning drive. And just like that, memories rushed into her mind of an awkward, lonely time in her life.

She'd been sixteen and upset about missing her high school dance. Not that she was much of a dancer, but she'd missed being with friends who seemed to be moving on without her. She wasn't happy spending most weekends on the road with Casey and this one Saturday night, she'd let her sour mood get the best of her.

Judd Calhoon and his friend were slightly older than she was and pretty much harmless. She wouldn't call Judd her friend. He'd mostly teased her about being scrawny and younger, but they'd shared one common complaint—both would rather be spending their weekends at home. So when he'd dared her to sneak out of the trailer that was her second home with Casey, Audrey had found herself eager and willing to thumb her nose at her big brother's rules. He was her half brother, anyway, she'd thought. And she'd been tired of his demanding, overprotective ways.

She'd met the boys at midnight—Casey, with a Saturday-night drunk on, would never have known she was gone—and they'd built a small campfire in a cleared-out field half a mile away from the rodeo arena. They'd had some laughs, and she'd been feeling really good about her rebellion. She'd even taken a swallow or two of whiskey the boys had brought along. Before she knew it, Judd's friend had passed out, falling into a snoring heap on the ground three feet away from her. Judd had been drinking heavily by then, and his usual mocking tone had suddenly turned affectionate. His hands got grabby and his pockmarked face was suddenly all over hers. Judd Calhoon, the brother of the rodeo clown, was no Romeo, and Audrey had shoved him away, telling him he was stupid for trying such a stunt.

Judd hadn't taken no for an answer. His affection had turned to demand and before Audrey knew it, she'd been pinned to the ground under him. "Get off," she'd said, shoving at him.

He was too big, too clumsy and too strong for her and she'd realized he'd *let* her shove him away the first time. This time, her shove didn't budge him.

"Aw, come on, Audrey. No one will know."

He'd smelled of whiskey and tobacco. He'd kissed her chin, her cheek and kept missing her mouth because he'd been drunk and because Audrey kept turning her face away as fast as he came at her. "I said get off," she'd shouted again, her fists pummeling the wooden block of his chest.

And he'd complied, just like that. Only it hadn't been Judd doing the moving, but Luke, his hands in a vise grip on Judd's shoulders. The next thing she knew, Judd was flying through the air, and Luke's face was red with fury when he'd gone after him. He'd picked Judd up where he'd landed and had held him by the scruff of the collar. He'd spoken with deadly calm then. Audrey, knowing Luke like she did, had realized his great restraint as he'd lectured Judd and placed the fear of God in him.

"You okay?" Luke had asked her after he was through with Judd. He'd helped her up and she'd dusted herself off, grateful to Luke, but fearing what he had to say to her, too.

"I'm f-fine."

"I wasn't gonna do anything to her, I swear," Judd's voice squeaked from the darkness.

Luke hadn't taken his eyes off her. "Shut up or I'll take you to the sheriff."

Luke had taken her hand then and led her to his truck. She'd gotten in and sat in silence on the ride back. She could tell Luke was fuming and part of his anger was aimed at her.

"That was real dumb going off in the middle of the night."

"I kn-know."

"Dangerous, too. Those boys are losers. Stupid to boot."

Audrey had nodded again.

Luke had killed the engine of his truck twenty feet away from the trailer she shared with Casey.

"Why'd you do it, Audrey Faith?"

She'd stared straight ahead into the night and opened up her heart, telling him about her loneliness, her sadness over missing her friends at school and her terrible boredom at the rodeo. She'd told him how Casey was all over her with rules and regulations and that she'd felt like she never fit with anyone, anywhere. How Casey was only her half brother and how she'd had half a life. She was rarely home when it mattered and her only salvation was her love of horses. She'd cried a few times and Luke had leaned over to wipe her tears tenderly with his kerchief.

She'd spilled her guts and Luke had nodded like he understood, giving her words of encouragement for her to let it all out. He'd truly listened to her and in the end, when her body sagged, spent from her crushing confessions and soulful tears, Luke had offered her a compromise. He wouldn't tell Casey what happened, and he'd go back to Judd and his friend and make sure they never bothered her again, if Audrey would promise to come to him when she was feeling like doing something stupid or reckless or dangerous. He'd encouraged her to talk to Casey about everything that bothered her, but told her he'd be there if she ever needed him.

For a girl who'd thought her brother would ground her for life if he ever found out what she'd done, Luke had offered her a dream deal. She'd agreed to his terms and Luke had sealed their little pact with a brotherly kiss to the cheek.

Audrey wasn't sure a girl of sixteen knew a darn thing about love, but she was ninety-nine percent certain that that was the night she'd fallen deeply and wholeheartedly in love with Lucas Slade.

Audrey stepped out of the shower and toweled off vigorously, purging the memory from her mind. She dabbed at her throat, chin and face and talked herself out of any more reminiscing. It wouldn't help her current situation. She was at a loss here with Luke.

And ten minutes away from making his lunch.

"You are in a pickle, Audrey," she muttered as she dressed in her only change of clothes.

She combed her hair, banding it in a ponytail, and glanced in the mirror. The clothes were a slight improvement over the ones she'd worn this morning—new black jeans hugged her hips below the waist and a white peasant's blouse with short sleeves sloped on her shoulders. Her boots were dark tan and well broken in, the most comfortable shoes she owned.

With three minutes to spare, she closed the door on her sleepy cat and sashayed down the hall, heading to the kitchen wondering if the old cliché still held true. The way to a man's heart was through his stomach. If only…

* * *

"Hey," Luke said as she entered the kitchen. His head was poking inside the fridge as he perused the shelves. "We've got leftover roast beef, turkey, ham and three different kinds of cheeses. It figures. I'm in the mood for a patty melt."

As Audrey breezed by him, she picked up the lime scent of his aftershave and refused to let it give her heart failure. Luke smelled good. Period. She'd have to get over it or she'd make a fool of herself. "I'll make you a patty melt. It'll be the rich man's version."

His mouth curved up. "What's that?"

"Wait and see, big man."

Luke laughed and sat at the granite island counter, watching her cook.

She found a fry pan, sweet butter, bread crumbs and sesame seed buns. It wasn't rocket science, but she was pretty darn proud of her creation when she was all through heating small chunks of roast mixed with bread crumbs and layered with melted cheese. The patty came together and she plopped it into a bun with a spatula. "Here you go."

Luke glanced at the dish she slid his way and cocked a brow. "I'm not that rich, by the way."

"Yes, you are." He was wealthy by anyone's standards with his shared ownership of Sunset Lodge and Sunset Ranch and, from Casey's accounting, half a dozen other investments. "But I won't hold that against you. Eat up."

He picked up the bun and dived in, taking a big bite. His eyes closed slowly and his face settled into an expression of sublime pleasure. "It'll do," he said.

"I thought so."

He took two more bites before his gaze slid back to her. "You having one?"

She shook her head. "I'll stick to a cheese sandwich."

He drew his brows together. "That's no fun, honey."

She couldn't get excited about an endearment he'd used in his usual brotherly tone.

"You're doing fine without me." He'd gobbled up the entire sandwich while sitting on a stool at the counter. "I'll make you another one, if you'd like."

He contemplated his empty plate, then gave two pats to a rock-solid stomach a quarter would bounce off. "Tempting, but I'd better not. Sophia and Logan are bringing us dinner tonight. And she's cooking up one of her specialties."

Us? They'd be a foursome tonight, but it would hardly be a double date. "I heard Logan was getting married."

"Yep. My brother's getting the better end of the deal, if you ask me."

She remembered how Logan would come to see Luke at the rodeo and they'd give each other a world of grief. It was all in good fun, for the most part, except when it wasn't. But even though they teased each other unmercifully, Audrey saw the love they had for each other. They'd have each other's backs if there was ever a problem. "Logan's quite a catch. I bet Sophia feels pretty lucky. I can't wait to meet her."

"You will in a few hours."

She placed a bun in the fry pan, then added a slab of cheese and a fresh slice of tomato. Luke walked over to the fridge again and pulled out a pitcher of lemonade. He poured two glasses and handed her one. He stood close, watching the cheese melt onto the bun as he sipped his drink. A trickle of moisture slipped down her neck. Just being near Luke made her break out in a sweat.

"What are you doing after you eat that?"

She shrugged. "I have no plans."

"I was gonna wait until tomorrow, but if you're up to it, I thought I'd take you over to meet Trib."

"Ah...the horse that nearly killed you."

"An exaggeration. There were a few broken ribs."

"He broke your right arm, too."

Luke stared at her. "I see your brother filled you in on my injuries."

Yes, Casey had told her afterward, but she'd also had first-hand knowledge of his broken arm in the cast. But mercy, the man had left-hand skills that satisfied her just fine.

"You had a concussion, too."

"But I'm right as rain now."

It was permission to look him over from top to bottom. Not that she didn't already know how *right* the man was. From the top of his sandy-blond hair down to his black snakeskin boots, Luke was perfect. "I'm glad you've recovered."

"Wasn't ever any doubt, but thanks. Appreciate it."

She took the last bites of her sandwich and rubbed shoulders with Luke, who insisted on helping with the mess. They tidied up the kitchen, cleaned the counters and put the plates away in the dishwasher before heading outside.

A few minutes later, Luke led Audrey to a distant stable, one built for special cases like Tribute, a stallion with great ancestry and beautiful grace, but temperamental as all get-out. The ranch hands had nicknamed him Tribulation for all the darn trouble the horse gave them on a daily basis. One day Luke thought he'd broken the damn horse's barriers and had let down his guard. That was the day Trib had sent him to the hospital.

"I don't want you near him unless I'm with you," Luke said. They walked out of the bright sunlight and into the much cooler barn. Even before he laid eyes on the dang horse, he heard the sound of his shuffling in his stall. "He isn't keen we're here. Darn horse is antisocial."

Audrey's eyes widened as she mentally accepted the challenge that Luke wouldn't let her near the horse until he felt it was safe. He wouldn't put her in danger, and Casey would probably crush him into pulp, anyway, if Luke let his kid sister get injured.

While she was staying at the ranch, Luke was responsible for her safety. He wouldn't take that lightly. Casey's trust was one reason, but Luke had always had a soft spot in his heart for her. If he'd had a sister, he'd want her to be just like Audrey Faith.

"You know I can't get much done with you hovering over me, Luke."

"I know no such thing. You can work your magic, with me *hovering* in the back of the barn. It's the only way I'll allow it."

"Now you sound like Casey. Bossy."

He had to smile at that. Casey was a pill when it came to his sister. "Maybe so, but just so we're clear, you're not to come in here unless I'm with you. Got that?"

Audrey frowned but finally nodded. "Okay."

They came up to the paddock at the far end of the barn and looked over the half door to see the stallion pacing and snorting. The space was larger than most, the ground covered with a bedding of cedar shavings and straw.

"He's a beauty," Audrey whispered in awe. Her expressive eyes lit with longing and Luke could see her mind working already. She would find a way to connect with this animal.

"That, he is. I hate to give up on him. I was tempted, believe me. After I tripped in the stall and cursed loud enough for the next county to hear me, Trib got perplexed, and it was all I could do to get out of his way before he trampled the stuffing out of me. He's got heralded ancestry and he'll make someone a fine horse one day. If—and that's a big if—we can find his gentle side."

The horse stayed near the back wall, looking at them with sharp, wary eyes that took everything in. He knew Luke, but he still didn't trust him. And now Audrey was added to the mix. "He's better in the corral, but he doesn't play well with others, so he's pretty much a loner."

"That has to change and it will. In time."

"You have a couple of months."

Audrey glanced at him. "It's a tall order, but I'll do my best." Her eyes deepened in color and her voice rang with sincerity. "I know this is important to you, Luke."

She was sweet, and he was grateful for her help. On impulse, he bent to kiss her cheek, but she shifted her head at that exact moment and damn if he didn't lay a kiss right smack on her mouth.

His senses filled. Her lips were soft and smooth against his rough mouth. She tasted familiar, like wild berries in the spring. She had a scent that lingered, reminding him of something he couldn't quite grasp. She purred deep in her throat, the sound a little startled and a whole lot of sexy. It made him wince and question his sanity as he pulled away sooner than he would've liked.

It was a short, quick kiss, but he'd learned this much: Audrey wasn't a delicate child. She was passionate. But when he wanted to explore a little more, the words CASEY'S SISTER flashed through his mind like a banner being pulled across the sky by a plane.

What was it Casey had said? She'd had a loser boyfriend and was feeling a little low right now. He couldn't take advantage of that.

"Sorry," he said quietly.

Audrey's expressive eyes stayed on his as seconds ticked by. Silence filled the barn. Not even Trib made a sound, and then finally she whispered, "No need to apologize."

"I meant to kiss your cheek."

"I know."

It had been an awkward head-shifting and lips-meshing moment. He couldn't put his finger on what niggled at him, but there was definitely something rattling around in his brain. He took a deep breath, noticing for the first time how unique Audrey's scent was. "Are you wearing perfume?"

She shook her head. "Lip gloss. It's called Sweet and Wicked."

Luke zeroed in on her mouth. He should've known. He'd taken a sip from her sweet and wicked lips and liked how she tasted.

"TMI?" she asked with a raised brow.

Too much information. Luke grinned. "Nope. Trust me, I can handle sweet and wicked."

Her eyes left his, but not before Luke caught an odd expression cross her features. "I figured as much."

Luke took a last glance at Trib in the paddock. The horse continued to watch them with a ready-to-bolt stance. "He's sizing us up."

"Together, we're too intimidating for him," Audrey said.

"He'll have to get used to it. From now on, it's him and you and me."

She sighed, and the warmth of her delicious breath wafted by his nostrils. He had a bad feeling that Sweet and Wicked would haunt his dreams tonight. But he kept that thought to himself as he laid a hand to the small of her back and led Audrey out of the barn.

After spending time with Luke, Audrey needed to calm her nerves. She lay down beside Jewel on the bed and the cat immediately started purring loud enough to wake the dead.

"You're happy to see me, aren't you?" she cooed. "Well, I'm happy to see you, too."

She stroked the back of Jewel's head, just under the ears. The cat's coat was soft and smooth under her fingertips. When she had enough, Jewel stretched her neck so that Audrey could scratch her under the chin and the cat's noisy purring settled into a soft hum.

The lull made Audrey's eyes grow heavy and she relaxed on the bed. Rather than fight it, she gave in to her fatigue by closing her eyes and then drifting off to sleep.

Later, the sound of a woman's voice outside her bedroom door startled her. "Audrey?"

Disoriented, Audrey lifted her head from the pillow.

Next came a soft knocking. The cat jumped down from the bed and padded to the door, listening. "Audrey? It's Sophia, Logan's fiancée. Are you okay in there?"

Audrey shook out the cobwebs from her head and glanced at the clock. It was after seven! She scrambled off the bed and strode to open the door. Audrey faced a stunning woman dressed in a summery, soft peach, spaghetti-strapped dress. She had long flowing dark hair, amber eyes and skin that could have been kissed by a Mediterranean sun. "Oh, hi."

"Hello. I'm sorry if I interrupted your sleep."

Audrey's hand flew to her disheveled hair that had come loose from the rubber band. Some people had hat hair. Audrey had bed hair and she could only imagine what the tangled mess sitting atop her head looked like right now. She wasn't brave enough to glance in the mirror. She straightened out a few wrinkles in her clothes for what it was worth. "I usually never sleep in the afternoon."

The woman smiled. "I'm Sophia."

"Audrey Faith Thomas. But everyone calls me Audrey." She stuck out her hand and instead of a shake, Sophia wrapped both hands over hers and gave a little squeeze.

"It's nice to meet you."

"Did I miss dinner?"

"Not at all," Sophia said. "Luke got a little worried when you didn't come down so I offered to check on you."

"I'm fine, just a little more tired than usual. Sorry to delay the meal." Audrey opened the door wider. "Come in. I just want to put a brush to this mop."

Sophia stepped into the room and Audrey rummaged around until she came up with her hairbrush. "I didn't bring too many clothes with me. My friend's sending my things from Reno, but unfortunately, for now, what you see is what you get."

"There's nothing wrong with the way you look," Sophia said. "Dinner is pretty casual at the Slades' these days."

She immediately liked Logan's fiancée. She was honest and didn't try to convince Audrey that she looked perfect or wonderful or beautiful, although Sophia was every single one of those things. "Congratulations on your engagement."

"Thank you. Logan's a pretty great guy." Sophia's lips curved into a mischievous smile. "Except when he wasn't."

Audrey laughed. "I hear you. Luke told me that you once hated each other."

"Hate's a strong word. And it was mostly him being stubborn, but we've gotten past that now. We're very much in love."

"Sounds nice. Like you two were meant for each other."

"I think we were. We've worked through our difficulties and now we're getting married. Honestly, I never thought this day would come."

Audrey sighed as she combed through her hair, battling with a knot here and there. She and Luke didn't have any difficulties. He didn't regard her as anything but a longtime friend. There was no great passion, no love/hate relationship. He'd kissed her today, just a peck on the lips, but it had still been glorious, and Audrey was ready for more. Yet his only reaction had been to apologize.

He didn't remember he'd made love to her. The memory constantly bounced in and out of her brain. It hurt like hell. And reminded her daily what a hopeless case she was.

Starting at the top of her head, she pushed both hands through her hair and roped the mane at the nape of her neck with a rubber band. Her mass of blond curls tapered into a ponytail that reached the middle of her back. "There."

"You have beautiful hair," Sophia said.

"Thanks, but it's a bit long. I've been thinking of having it cut."

"I know of a good hair salon in town when you decide."

"That would be great."

They walked to the kitchen together, and Audrey's steps lightened as she spoke with Sophia Montrose. She was genuinely nice and put Audrey at ease. She shared a little bit about how she'd come to Sunset Ranch in the first place. Sophia had led a very intriguing life before she settled here with Logan. Audrey was eager to hear more, but when they reached the kitchen, the conversation ended. Two gorgeous Slade men sitting at the kitchen table rose from their seats when they walked in. It was a sweet gesture women didn't see very often anymore.

Her gaze locked onto Luke and she met with his bluer than blue eyes. Heart hammering, her breaths came quick. She cursed silently and struggled to quell her jittery nerves.

"There they are," Logan said as he walked over to her. "Good to see you again, Audrey." He gave her a hug and then flashed a brilliant smile. He was a dark-haired, dark-eyed version of Luke, and just as devilishly handsome.

"It's good to see you, too."

"Pip-squeak's going on twenty-five. Can you believe it?" Luke intervened.

"Tell me he doesn't call you that," Logan said.

Audrey would have been mortified if she didn't know Luke was just poking fun. Luke had never called her that. When Casey would, Luke would tell him to show some respect. She sent Luke her fiercest glare. "Not if he wants to live to tell about it."

Luke busted out laughing. "She means it, too." He winked at her, just like he did when she was a kid.

Logan took Sophia by the hand and drew her into his arms. "I see you met my soon-to-be wife." He kissed her cheek. "You two get acquainted?"

"We did, a little." Sophia glanced at her with warmth in her eyes.

Audrey smiled back.

"Are you ready to sit down to eat?" Sophia asked. "I made paella Valenciana. I hope you like it, Audrey. It's my mother's recipe and Logan loves it."

"It's one of my favorites, too," Luke said. "I can't wait to dig in."

"It smells delicious," Audrey said. The flavorful scent of saffron and spices rose up to tickle her senses. She peeked at the concoction on the stove. A mixture of vegetables, rice, tomatoes and what looked like pork pieces filled a cast-iron skillet. "Can I help?"

"Sure," Sophia said. "Why don't you help me dish it into the plates and serve?"

"I'd love to do that." Audrey was glad to work beside Sophia in the kitchen. It made her feel like part of a family, like she belonged.

Audrey filled the plates for Luke and herself and set them onto the table while Sophia portioned out enough for her and Logan. "Audrey, if you could toss the salad, I'll put the bread on the table."

"I'd be happy to." Audrey took hold of the teak salad bowl and used the utensils to give the ingredients several good tosses. Once it was ready, she brought the salad over to the table set with earthen stoneware and very simple stainless-steel cutlery.

Luke opened a bottle of red wine. "Paella goes down easy with merlot." He poured wine into all four goblets and everyone took their seats. Sophia sat next to Logan, which left Audrey to sit beside Luke.

It wasn't a hardship being close to Luke. Somewhere between the paella and a half a glass of wine during the meal, her heartbeats had slowed to normal. The conversation was lively as she became better acquainted with the Slades and Sophia. She'd learned about Sophia and Luke's tight friendship as children and how Logan had felt left out and jealous about it. Sophia didn't go much further into detail but it was something Audrey was curious about. She planned on finding out more one day if Sophia was willing to share the information.

What a sucker she was. Or was she a glutton for punishment? Everything about Luke's life outside the rodeo fascinated her.

"Luke's still my best friend," Sophia said. Logan gave her a nod of approval. "And I hear he was like a big brother to you, too, Audrey."

Audrey gulped the last drop of her wine. Not the brother thing again. Mercy, she was tired of it, but Sophia was just making polite conversation and couldn't possibly know how much Audrey hated the subject, so she answered her with equal politeness. "Yes, when Casey wasn't around, Luke watched out for me."

She glanced at Luke and found him staring, his gaze focused and piercing. Was he remembering that night when he'd rescued her by the bonfire? The night he'd nearly flattened Judd Calhoon on her behalf. Was he remembering all the other times he'd been there for her? His eyes stayed on hers for a few long moments and then swept down to her mouth. Heat curled in her belly and a memory flashed of that nothing-yet-everything kiss from this afternoon.

"My brother is the Goody Two-shoes in the family," Logan said. "In this case, I'm glad he watched out for you two ladies."

"Hey," Luke said. "If a beautiful woman needs my help, I'm there."

A moment ticked by. Then it hit Audrey. Luke had called her beautiful.

Good gracious. She had to stop banking on his every word. It wasn't the first time he'd paid her a compliment. He was Mr. Nice Guy, she reminded herself.

After dinner, they had a second glass of wine, and though the men offered to help with the cleanup , Sophia shooed them into the family room to watch the baseball game.

"The paella was delicious," Audrey said, bringing the empty dishes to the counter next to the sink.

"Thank you. I'll share the recipe with you if you'd like."

"I would love that. I just don't know when I'd have time to try it out. Once my job is done here, I'll be starting veterinarian school again."

"Luke told us what you did for your brother when he broke his back. You dropped out of school to care for him."

"Casey needed me. I wouldn't have it any other way. He's done so much for me and it was the least I could do for him. Of course, I'd hate for him to hear me say that…he and I butt heads a lot."

Sophia rinsed the plates and nodded. "That's what family is all about." A hint of longing touched her voice. "I never had a brother or sister to butt heads with. Maybe that's why Luke and I became such good friends." Sophia was thoughtful for a few seconds, her gaze going somewhere distant. "My mother and I were very close, too. I miss her terribly."

Audrey understood great loss, yet she didn't know her folks enough to miss them with the kind of intensity she saw in Sophia's eyes. More like, Audrey missed the idea of her parents. She missed big Sunday dinners and Christmas mornings and having a mother to come home to after school, offering snacks and hugs. She missed having a father to teach her to ride a bike and kiss her forehead when she did her chores properly.

"I'm sorry to hear about your mother, Sophia. I didn't know my mom. She died when I was a baby, and shortly after, my father married Casey's mom. But we lost both of them in a horrible tornado that passed through our town in Oklahoma just a few years later. It touched down and swept away everything in its path over one square mile."

"Oh, that's awful," Sophia said, her eyes widening with horror.

It was the same incredulous reaction Audrey got when she

explained the circumstances of the tragedy to others. Usually she didn't like talking about it.

"How did you escape?"

"Casey and I were playing with friends on the other side of town. The tornado missed us. It's weird, you know. One side of a street could be completely destroyed, and the other could be eerily untouched."

Sympathy touched Sophia's eyes. "I've seen it on the news and always wondered how that could be."

"It was really hard and nightmarish on us, but we managed. We had no choice." Audrey shrugged then. Life had been tough after that, but Casey had always provided for them. He had uncanny talent as a bronc buster and had made more than enough money on the rodeo circuit to keep a roof over their heads and plenty of food on the table. Audrey didn't dwell on the past. She refused to spend her life feeling sorry for herself. "It's been Casey and me ever since."

Sophia smiled as she loaded the last of the dishes into the dishwasher. "I think we have a lot in common, Audrey. It'll be nice having another female living on the ranch again."

"I'm looking forward to it." Audrey really meant it. She'd been unnerved coming here to face Luke. She'd lost her courage in confronting him, but she'd gained something, too. A job and a chance to matter, doing something she loved to do. She was looking forward to working with Trib and the other horses, spending time on the ranch and getting to know Sophia better. "And who knows, we might just diffuse the toxic levels of testosterone around here."

Sophia laughed lightly. "We can certainly try. I think you and I are going to be great friends."

Her heart panged with warmth. She could use a new friend. "Me, too."

"Hey, everyone, I'd like you to meet Katherine Grady. She goes by Kat."

At the sound of Luke's voice, Audrey whirled toward the

kitchen door. A Marilyn Monroe look-alike with platinum-blond hair stood beside him, her wide green eyes fashionably made-up to match her pretty emerald-and-blue outfit. She held on to Luke's arm and darn if Audrey didn't hone right in on that. A flashback of rodeo groupies—pouty pink lips and all—came to mind. Her heart sank. She struggled to keep her expression from taking a nosedive in front of everybody.

"Nice to meet you," Kat said, her voice soft as butter.

Suddenly, Audrey's head clouded up and spun. It was like the time she'd climbed onto the mechanical bull at Dusty's Dancehall in Texas. She'd been sixteen and trying to prove to the guys she wasn't a child. As soon as the bull started bucking, everything in that honky-tonk got blurry real fast. Only this was worse.

The world around her began to fade. Her legs went numb. She reached forward to grip the kitchen counter and missed, scraping her fingernails on the sharp edges. Desperate to hold on, her arms flailed. She needed support. But it was too late.

Blackness surrounded her.

Right before all the lights went out.

Three

Audrey woke to Luke hovering over her. Her body was flattened out on the Slade kitchen floor and her head ached like crazy. She blinked and stared into his concerned eyes as the palm of his hand rested on her hot face. Her cheeks stung, so she figured she'd been slapped a time or two. Relief filled his voice when he spoke to her. "Audrey Faith, you gave us a scare."

She tried to lift her head up. Two Lukes appeared in her line of vision. She blinked one of them away and as she eased back down, Luke's other hand cushioned her head. "How long was I out?" she asked quietly.

"Not long. Does this happen often?" he asked.

"This was the first time," she said, feeling a little bit ridiculous. Four pairs of eyes—including the blonde woman's—ogled her.

"You fainted." Sophia spoke softly, holding a bottle of smelling salt in her hand. "Luke rushed over to you. He got to you before we had to use this. It was just a few seconds."

A few seconds too many, she thought.

"What happened, honey?" Luke asked.

"I'm not sure. I got light-headed. Then everything went black."

"Logan's calling the doctor," Sophia said.

"Oh, no. I don't need a doctor." Audrey made a move to sit up again and when twin Lukes didn't appear, she figured she was good to go. His hand to her back, he helped hinge her forward slowly. "My head's not spinning anymore. I think… it's just…"

What was it? She didn't know why she'd fainted. It couldn't have been because Kat showed up attached to Luke at the hip. She'd seen Luke with other women before. No amount of nose twitching would make them disappear, though. And as a smitten teen, she'd daydream of trading places with the females on his arm. Audrey knew that this time it wasn't Kat's presence that made her see stars.

She'd been overly tired today and a little stressed. A reasonable excuse came to mind. "I might've caught a bug or something."

"Now I'm sorry I woke you up for dinner," Sophia said, her expression grim. "You probably needed your sleep."

Logan entered the room with the phone to his ear. "I can't get hold of the doctor. Maybe we should take her to emergency."

Luke nodded. "Good idea."

"No, it's not necessary." Audrey summoned all of her strength, planted her feet and rose to full height, refusing Luke's extended arm for support. There. She wasn't dizzy anymore. Whatever happened had been freakish, but it had passed. "I feel better already. I think all I need is a good night's sleep. It's a bug and I need to rest. Honestly." She glanced at Logan first, then at Luke, giving him a pointed look. No way was she going to disrupt their evening by going to the hospital. Besides, she really did feel better.

The men darted glances at each other. "What do you think?" Luke said to Logan.

"I'm fine," she said a little more firmly.

Logan shrugged. "She looks fine, Luke."

Sophia added, "You can check on her during the night, Luke."

Kat, who had been quiet throughout this exchange, raised a perfectly arched brow at that.

"You sure you're feeling okay?" Luke asked, his genuine concern touching something deep and lasting in her heart. As if she needed another reason to worship him.

She nodded, did a pirouette right in the middle of the kitchen—ending with a flourish a gymnast would be proud of—and gave him a big smile. "I promise I'm okay."

"As long as I've got your promise, we're good. I'll walk you to your room."

She wanted to protest. She could walk to her own room, for heaven's sake, but the envious look in Kat Whoever-she-was's eyes made her accept his invitation. "Sure."

She turned to Sophia and Logan, giving them each a big hug. And then, magnanimously, she put out her hand to Kat. "So good to meet you," she said, as if she hadn't just made a spectacle of herself by fainting.

"I hope you're feeling better soon." Kat cupped her hand and gave a little squeeze,

Audrey's gaze shifted to her white knight. "If Luke has anything to say about it, I will."

The comment flew over the men's heads, but Sophia had a glint in her eye as Luke walked Audrey out of the kitchen.

Once they reached her bedroom, Luke turned the knob and opened the door. "I'll check in on you later."

"Not necessary, really."

"I'm gonna insist, Audrey."

She didn't like the idea of Luke coming to her room during the night. Well, okay, she would like the idea if his motives were different. Regardless of his friendship with Casey, she wasn't his obligation. She could fend for herself. He didn't need to lose sleep over her.

When she paused for a moment he added, "Your welfare is my responsibility as long as you're under my roof. You fainted tonight. We don't know why."

"I told you why."

"You're guessing, but you don't know for sure."

He wasn't letting this drop. Mr. Nice Guy was also a Good Samaritan.

An idea popped into her head. "How about if you text me?"

He chuckled from deep in his throat and a boyish gleam lit his eyes. "You're sleeping three doors down."

"It could be fun. And you don't have to be disturbed."

Luke rolled his eyes. "Fine, I'll text you. I've got your number."

"Great. Well then, good night."

"Sleep tight, Audrey."

After closing the door to Luke, her lungs released a whoosh of air, and she slumped against the door as the last bit of her energy seeped out. She was more tired than she'd let on to the Slades. She'd never fainted before. What was that all about? She chalked it up to emotional angst seeing Luke again. By all rights she should feel exhausted after the highs and lows she experienced today. The lowest was finding out that Luke had no memory of their night together. That had been a crushing blow, and she hadn't been allowed time to absorb the implications and heal her wounded heart and deflated ego.

Audrey undressed with deliberately slow moves, carefully peeling off her clothes. No sense tempting fate. A sudden move here or there and she might find herself on the floor again without a dashing prince to awaken her.

She hung up her blouse in a double-wide closet and folded her jeans in half, putting them across a captain's chair in the corner of the room. She washed her face and brushed her teeth, then climbed into bed, giving Jewel a little nudge. "Why aren't you a curl-up kind of cat?"

The cat was stretched out, taking up most of the width of the bed, and the prod moved her only enough to give Audrey room to climb in. She sank into the comfort awarded her in that small space. She picked up the remote control and clicked on the television. Mindless babbling might just comfort her to sleep tonight. She settled on a reality show that Susanna constantly raved about. Her friend, the reality-show junkie, watched them all and had recommended this one specifically for Audrey.

"Wannabes and Wranglers," Audrey mumbled, sinking into the pillow.

The first ten minutes entertained her enough to keep watching the city slickers trying to replicate life in a mock-up Western town. Poor John Wannabe was having trouble saddling up his horse. He got the cinch all wrong and the saddle might have slipped off if it weren't for Wrangler Beth, who'd come to the rescue. They were teamed up for a series of challenges and it was Beth's job to turn John into a horseman in less than two months. John was halfway into his on-camera, heartfelt confession explaining how Beth made him nervous because she was so beautiful when Audrey's cell phone barked. The *ruff-ruff* ringtone had Jewel lifting her head sharply to listen. "It's just a text," she explained to her cat.

She picked up her phone from the nightstand and read Luke's message.

Are you sleeping yet?

She punched in an answer.

Obviously not.

What are you doing?

Watching *Wannabes and Wranglers*. I'm fine.

A few seconds later, another text came through.

Glad you're fine. I'm watching that, too.

Really? Luke watched reality shows? She found that hard to believe.

Because Beth is so hot?

It only took a few seconds for Luke to respond.

Yes.

Then a few moments later:

But I like the concept, too.

What do you think of John?

she texted, closing her eyes briefly after typing in the question.
His next text came instantly.

Not a fast learner.

Audrey smiled as she punched in her reply.

He's distracted by Beth.

So am I. She knows her way around a stallion.

Hardy, har-har. Look, John finally got the horse saddled right. Beth's teaching him how to mount.

That should come naturally to a man.

Was he teasing? She immediately wrote back,

A woman, too, if the stallion's worthy.

An image flashed through her mind of her mounting Luke and taking them both for a sweet ride. His hips had arched and he'd bucked from underneath, meeting her every stride with a fierceness that penetrated her body and soul. The notion layered through her belly in warm waves.

His next text came through.

Mounting a horse, I meant.

Right. You don't fool me, Luke.

I never did. You almost ready to turn in?

Yes. Go to sleep. I'm fine.

Lights out.

I've already done that once tonight.

Funny. Wake me if you need me, Audrey.

That was a loaded comment and a dozen *needs* regarding Luke flitted through her mind.

Night, Luke.

Night.

Well, it wasn't text sex or anything close, but Audrey turned off the television and fell fast asleep with a big smile on her face.

* * *

At seven o'clock the next morning, Audrey was greeted with another text from Luke.

Are you up yet?

She was never one to sleep late.

Up and dressed,

she keyed into the phone and then added,

Feeling fine.

Not five seconds later, Luke was knocking on her bedroom door. "That was fast," she muttered, tossing her phone down on the bed to pull the door open.

He leaned against the door frame, eyeing her from top to bottom, doing a clean sweep and making her wish she'd had something to wear besides her faded jeans and oversize shirt. At least she'd managed to put a comb through her hair and pull it back into a ponytail.

Luke came to her freshly shaven, with that same hint of lime wafting in the air, his longish clean hair curling at the ends. One strand slashed across his forehead to rest on his brow. Audrey mentally sighed. The crisp tight fit of his jeans and snug hug of a dark blue canvas shirt were enough to still her heart. "Mornin'."

"Hi."

"Sleep well?"

"Very well." It was no lie.

"No fainting spells today?"

"None, and I feel great."

Luke's lips twisted downward. "Do me a favor and don't do that again."

"You don't have to keep checking on me."

"I came to deliver a message. Breakfast is ready. Cereal and toast. *Unless*..."

"Unless...I cook up something better?"

"You *can* stir a pot and I'm hungry."

"When are you not? How does bacon and eggs over easy sound?"

"Throw in half a dozen buttermilk pancakes and we've got a deal."

"Okay, but only if you admit you opened my door last night to peek in on me."

He crossed his arms over his chest and planted his feet firmly. "I'm admitting nothing."

"What kind of cereal do you want?"

Luke's shoulders drooped and he sighed. "Okay, fine. I peeked in on you."

Food blackmail always worked.

"I slept better knowing Casey's little sister was sleeping soundly."

She did a mental eye roll. How old did she have to be before Luke stopped thinking of her as Casey's younger sister? "You make the coffee...I'm assuming you know how...and I'll get to work on the rest."

"It's a deal."

The cat jumped down from the bed, took a long stretch and strode over to Luke. She rubbed her body along his legs and bowed her back like a rainbow, purring loudly. Audrey could take a lesson or two in flirting from her cat.

Luke bent to scratch her under the chin. "I think it's time Miss Jewel got out of this room."

"I agree. I was going to ask if it's okay if she roams around the ranch today."

"Yeah, no problem. She's probably smart enough to stay out of trouble."

"She's only used up one of her nine lives. She's got eight more to go."

With that, they headed to the kitchen. During breakfast, Luke mentioned Kat again and Audrey asked him about her. "She's just a friend" was all he said with a shrug of the shoulder.

Audrey figured the woman would never forget her, though. She'd made a lasting impression. How many people fainted the second they were introduced?

After breakfast, Luke gave her a grand tour of the ranch and explained her duties as wrangler. She was to groom and exercise the horses, make sure they were fed properly and assist the head wrangler, Ward Halliday. They wouldn't be working with Trib today, and that was fine with her because she had some shopping to do in town when she finished up her duties.

Luke left her in the barn with Hunter Halliday, Ward's son, who was leaving for college in a few weeks. The big, strapping boy with a friendly smile showed her around the barn and introduced her to each one of the ranch hands during the course of the day. They were nice men who spoke politely and had nothing but respect for the horses on the property.

"We don't sell a horse every day," Hunter said. "Sometimes, only one or two a week, but once they go, you miss them. It's best if you ride them and train them and try not to get close to them. The Slades take care with who they sell a horse to. You gotta tell yourself they're going to a good home."

Hunter used a currycomb on the mare he was grooming while Audrey stood up on a footstool and braided a thoroughbred's mane, something she'd learned to do when she was thirteen. "I volunteer at a horse rescue at home. I know it's not easy saying goodbye."

Hunter nodded.

They worked together on the horses into the morning. Jewel pretty much stayed by her side in the barn, sitting up regally and taking swipes at the flies buzzing around her head. It seemed to keep her entertained. And for the remainder of the morning, they took horses out that hadn't been exercised yesterday. Hunter showed her different paths to follow and made sure the horses got a good workout before they switched them out. More grooming followed and by midafternoon their work was done.

Audrey's clothes stuck to her body and the skin exposed to the hot sun was layered with a fine coating of trail dust. Her mouth could spit cotton, as Casey would say, and her bones ached a little, but she'd never been happier.

She was in her element.

After her work was done, she hummed her way back to the house with Jewel in her arms. "You earned your keep today," she said. "Those dang flies didn't stand a chance."

The shower she took was quick and efficient, cleansing her body of barn grime, and within minutes, Audrey was clean and ready to go.

She had a shopping date with Sophia this afternoon.

"Sophia, I can't possibly wear all of these things." Draped over Audrey's arms and threatening to topple her were two pairs of slacks, three pairs of designer jeans, four blouses, a stylish leather jacket and, so that all was not lost, a skimpy cherry-red thong swimsuit that Audrey wouldn't think of ever wearing out in public.

"Nonsense," Sophia said, eyeing another item from the rack in Sunset Lodge's gift shop. "You can't have too many clothes." Sophia added a pair of white studded jeans to the pile dangling from her arms. "They're a gift from Logan, Luke and me."

"Do they know about this?"

Sophia's chuckle came out warm and friendly. "They give me carte blanche with the gift shop. Neither one of them has ever had anything to do with it."

Audrey understood why. The place was a virtual one-stop shop with classic designer items like sequined evening bags, ladies apparel and jewelry that fit with the Western theme of Sunset Ranch. Over in the corner was one small shelf stacked with men's shirts that were manly enough for any cowboy to wear. Everything was tastefully displayed and organized to appeal to the eye. In short, Sophia's stamp of approval was written all over it.

"This is very sweet of you," Audrey said, humbled by her generosity.

"It's my pleasure. I think you've got some things that'll dazzle."

"Yeah, the horses at the barn are gonna love me in them."

Sophia smiled and began searching the shop further. What could she possibly add to this wardrobe?

"No, I wasn't thinking about the horses," Sophia said. "Here, let me take those from you." She scooped her arms under the pile weighing Audrey down and carried the clothes to the counter by the cash register. "I'll put them aside and have them wrapped for you. After I take you on a tour of the lodge, we can swing by here and pick them up."

"Thank you." Audrey didn't have words enough to express her gratitude.

Sophia spoke to a young girl assisting behind the counter and then they exited the shop. Sophia guided her into the lobby, past the massive stone fireplace that greeted every guest who entered the lodge. Wood beams overhead and sandstone floors and comfortable sitting areas were set off by big windows and a natural elegantly rustic setting.

"I don't remember ever coming here. I've only been to the ranch a few times when I was younger but we never stopped by the lodge. This is a beautiful spot. It's got a rural feel, but it's up-to-date, too. I like the combination of old and new."

"I know what you mean. My mother used to manage the lodge when I was a kid. She was proud to work here."

"I can see why."

"I'm glad I came back. A part of me never left," Sophia said, her eyes darkening with memories.

It was the opening Audrey needed to ask a question that had been burning inside. It was none of her beeswax, but that didn't stop her. She had a compelling desire to learn about the Slades, Luke in particular.

"And Logan wasn't happy about it initially?"

"No, he wasn't thrilled when I showed up here. He and I had prior history going back to our childhood and he resented me inheriting half ownership of the lodge from the Slades. His father...well, Randall Slade was more than generous with me. It's no secret," she said as they stopped by a large picture window that overlooked the grounds, "that I loved living at Sunset Ranch. I grew up here, but things got complicated for my mom and we moved away. It wasn't until I came back that I was forced to confront Logan and my feelings for him. After fighting with each other and holding back our feelings, we finally saw that we were meant to be together. We put the past behind us and it's stayed there. And through it all, Luke and I remained good friends."

"Were you and Luke...ever, uh—"

Audrey was dying to know. Had there been a heated love triangle among the Slade brothers and Sophia?

Sophia's head tilted with a negative shake. "Never. We don't think of each other that way. He's my friend. I'm his friend. It's never been anything more."

It was hard to believe. How could anyone be that close to Luke and not fall madly in love with him? Was she the only hopeless case around here?

They walked to the kitchen and Sophia introduced her to Constance, young Edward's grandmother, who was the head chef. She and the rest of the staff were busy preparing for the dinner meal. "I've met your grandson. He's a nice boy," she said.

"Thank you. I think so, too." Constance's warm smile told

Audrey that Edward was the apple of her eye. "Here, give this a try. I'm not sure it's quite right." She handed each one of them a pastry glazed with chocolate. "Tell me what you think. There's mocha crème filling inside."

Audrey took a bite and chocolate cream squirted into her mouth, hitting all the right sensory points. Her reaction was immediate and honest. "Yummy."

Sophia nodded, too, as she chewed. They were in agreement.

"That's what I was hoping to hear," Constance said.

After chatting and testing two more samples, they left the kitchen to head toward the stables. "These horses are for the guests," Sophia explained. "Hunter and Ward oversee their care as well as the horses at the ranch. We give guided tours and have hayrides and horseback-riding lessons. Most people who come here want to ride in some way or another."

Audrey had a chance to meet the horses that weren't already out with guests and bond a little with each one. A softly spoken word, a pat on the head or an affectionate nuzzle went a long way with animals.

"You're welcome anytime to hang out with them. I'm sure Ward would welcome it," Sophia said. "As you can see, they're gentle and sweet. We worry that sometimes they don't get enough attention."

"I'll visit them as often as I can." She stroked a palomino on the side of her face, looking into her warm brown eyes, and knew they would be fast friends.

A few minutes later, they returned for the clothes at the gift shop. Audrey was ready to put the packages in her pickup truck and give her thanks once again. Before she got the words out, Sophia tilted her head thoughtfully with a smile on her lips. "Logan and I are having a little engagement party next week. We'd love it if you joined us."

"You're inviting me to your engagement party?"

"Yes, it's for family and close friends. Please say you'll come."

Touched by the invitation, Audrey's heart warmed. "Oh, I… Of course. Thank you for including me. Just tell me where and when and I'll be there."

"I'll be sure to do that. I'll call you tonight."

"Okay." Audrey was almost out the door with the packages when Sophia called out. "Wait! I forgot this. I have one more thing for you."

Audrey's eyes grew wide when she saw what Sophia had in her hand. "You… I can't… What am I going to do with that?"

"Isn't it beautiful?" she asked, her voice sweetly determined.

"It's gorgeous, but I sleep in an old T-shirt."

Sophia's eyes lit with amusement. "When you're alone, yes. But this is for that someone special."

The black negligee spoke of hot, raw, wicked sex. It wasn't your grandmother's negligee, she thought, and then laughed at the notion of grandmothers and hot sex. Where had her mind drifted? This nightie was cut low on the bosom, high on the thigh and was woven with intricate, peek-a-boo lace. It said *do me* in a hundred different languages. "I don't have someone special."

Sophia ignored her and boxed the negligee herself, giving it a light tap with the flat of her hands. "I think there's someone special for you on this ranch. I've seen the way you look at Luke."

"Luke?" She gulped air. Was she busted? "Luke and I aren't…anything. I mean…sure, he's been my brother's friend for ages, but—"

But what? She wasn't ready to divulge her secret to anyone, much less Luke's best friend. Oddly, Sophia didn't pry. She didn't try to get any further explanation out of her. She listened and nodded and then placed the box in her arms.

She had an uncanny feeling that Sophia Montrose was

wiser than her years. The alternative was that Audrey wasn't fooling anyone about her feelings for Luke. She preferred to think Sophia had especially sharp perception. "Please accept this as my personal gift to you."

"It's very kind of you."

"Wear it well and knock his socks off."

"I'm not knocking anyone's socks off," she said mildly, but her throat caught with the comment as an image of making love to Luke in that negligee popped into her head.

Sophia shrugged. "Then someone like Kat Grady might just turn Luke's head."

"I—I wouldn't know," she said, feeling glum. "I've only been upright about ten seconds in her presence."

Sophia's gaze stayed on her and a little smile emerged. "Luke was worried about you all evening."

"He feels responsible for me."

"He likes you."

"He thinks of me as a younger sister."

"Men can change their minds in the blink of an eye."

She was speaking of her experience with Logan. He'd hated Sophia and hadn't wanted her at the ranch. The irony wasn't lost on Audrey. She had the opposite problem. Luke had always liked her and had made her feel welcome here, giving her a job and offering his friendship. In a weird and crazy way, she had just as high a mountain to climb to make Luke look at her differently as Sophia had with Logan. "Who is Kat, anyway?"

Sophia shrugged one shoulder. "I don't know much about her. She's new to the county and settled in the next town, Silver Springs."

"She's very pretty, in a flashy sort of way," Audrey said.

"Luke's seen her a few times, but he won't get serious about her. She's got a little baby."

"That doesn't sound like Luke. I thought he liked kids."

"He loves kids. You see how he is with Edward. But he

doesn't want to start up something he can't finish, and getting involved with a single mother could hurt her little boy when it ended."

"How is he so sure it would end?"

"That you'd have to ask Luke about. But I will tell you that he's got this thing about long-term relationships. He says he'll know pretty quickly when it's right, and so far, that hasn't happened. He's usually the first one to walk away."

Audrey didn't want to read too much into it, because hope that faltered and died was worse than no hope at all. And Luke had topped her No Hope list for a long time. If she dared to hope, she could come out scarred for life, but then, wasn't that the whole reason she took the job here? To have some sort of chance with Luke? Sophia knew Luke better than anyone. Didn't she? And she seemed to be encouraging Audrey to muster up, dig in her heels and make a stand.

Yet, deep down she didn't think Luke would ever see her as anything but a friend. Maybe he thought of her in the same way he thought of Sophia. There was a line he wouldn't cross with their friendship. Just like the line he refused to cross with the Grady woman.

Oh, who was she kidding?

Audrey, you are making excuses for your cowardice.

It was true. She was a coward.

She hadn't fessed up to Luke about seducing him and then running off like a frightened juvenile. She hadn't spilled the truth to him when she'd first arrived at the ranch. She hadn't been brave enough to look into Luke's trusting blue eyes and tell him what she'd done or why she'd done it. There'd been a few really good opportunities to bring up the subject, like when Luke had accidentally kissed her or when he'd come to her bedroom door this morning to check on her.

"And you think I'm right for Luke?"

Sophia gave her shoulder a lift and Audrey held her breath waiting for her reply. What would be worse, if Sophia said no or if she said yes? "You could be. But if you don't give it a chance, you'll never know."

Sort of like, if you don't try, you can't fail, but then you're left with years of wondering what if. "Thank you for the beautiful negligee." And for the nudge that had her convinced she may lose her chance with Luke if she didn't act fast. Luke was eligible, handsome and a great guy. He was like a marked target and another Kat might come along and hit the bull's-eye if she wasn't careful. Audrey made a silent, determined vow to speak with Luke soon. Her cowardly days were numbered. "I, uh…I owe you."

Sophia laid a hand on her arm. Audrey valued the comfort and friendship offered. "I'm happy to do it. And you don't owe me a thing." Then a delicious twinkle brightened Sophia's eyes and she added, "But Luke might, one day."

Four

Luke watched Audrey from a short distance away from Trib's paddock. As long as she stayed on her side of the half door, she'd be safe.

"He sees you, Luke. Back up a bit."

Luke leaned against the shaded, wide double door of the barn. If he stepped any farther back, beams of sunlight flowing inside would get in his eyes and not allow him to see a thing. "This is as far as I'm going, Audrey. Deal with it."

Audrey turned to him. Honey-gold strands of hair bunched under her felt hat escaped their confinement and streaked across cheeks reddened by frustration. She kept her tone light, but hissed the words through barely parted lips. "You're not helping. He's wary. Two of us here is hard for him to take right now."

He answered her by crossing his arms over his chest.

Jutting her lower lip out, she blew the strands of hair off her face and whirled back around, giving him a pretty spectacular view of her backside. He grinned at the sequins forming twin diamond shapes on the pockets covering the firm mounds of her butt. She'd grumbled about the designer jeans all the way out here, but Luke thought they looked great on her. So did the tank top tucked inside, with the words *Cowgirls Know How to Ride* printed in hot pink on the front.

A strange fleeting jab affected him. His mind took a journey in search of something…something teetering on the edge of his memory. Something he couldn't put his finger on. But at odd moments like this, while focused on Audrey's sweet derriere, bizarre met with bewilderment in his head.

The same thing had happened when he'd kissed her the other day and he'd plagued his mind for the answer to a question he couldn't even fathom.

Weird.

Audrey used sweet, soothing words on the stallion. Her voice took on the tone of a lulling siren trying to coax Trib away from the back wall of his stable. Luke could easily fall victim to that melodic sweet tone. He absorbed the sound that calmed his own jittery nerves. Audrey was the best at patience and consistency. She earned trust. But it took time. She was hoping for a sign from the stallion. One step toward her would mean progress. Yet, the horse remained rooted to the spot, unyielding. His snorts were pensive and muted, like the quiet before the storm. Luke had been fooled by Trib once. He wouldn't let Audrey suffer the consequences of Trib's explosive temper.

"Luke, he won't come over to me with you standing there."

"You're losing your touch, Audrey." Such a lie.

"You're being unreasonable. Go away."

"I'll think about it tomorrow, Audrey. We should get going now."

"We just got here. You go. I'll stay."

Luke walked over to her. "He's in a mood today. You're not getting anywhere with him."

"Let me be the judge of that. If you leave, I promise I'll be right behind you in five minutes."

He shook his head.

"Five minutes, Luke." Her pretty eyes beseeched him.

He considered it for all of twenty seconds. Audrey's unfaltering gaze stayed homed in on his and it was all he could to do to stick to his guns.

"Not today. Don't rush it."

"I'm not rushing it. But I won't make progress unless you give me some leeway."

"Not at the expense of your safety."

"The stable is sturdy, right? The walls are intact. I'm not planning on going inside the stall."

"Damn straight you're not." In a second he'd lose his cool. He didn't have the patience of a saint and he was used to his employees obeying his orders. He glanced at his watch. "Crap. I'm running late. I've gotta go."

"Got a hot date or something?" Her face flamed with indignation. "Is that why you won't let me do my job?"

"Yes, I have a date." And he wasn't looking forward to it. Kat had pretty much insisted he come over for dinner tonight as a thank-you for helping sort through old stable gear, reins, bits and saddles at Matilda Applegate's run-down little homestead in Silver Springs. Kat had moved in to care for the older woman, who was recovering from a heart attack, and had made it her mission to straighten out the place.

The first time Luke met Kat, she'd been loaded down with grocery bags, hanging onto a sweet-looking little baby boy named Connor and all of his diaper gear. Luke had offered his help and they got to talking afterward. He learned that the boy's father was a marine who'd died overseas, and the man's aunt, Matilda Applegate, was Connor's only living relative. Kat didn't like talking about her loss and he hadn't pried, figuring the subject was taboo and probably extremely painful. Luke should have steered clear then, because the last thing Kat needed was another heartache in her life, so now he had some hard thinking to do. She was beautiful and nice, but there were no sparks.

An image flashed of the blonde mystery woman riding atop him, sucking every last drop of juice from his body. He should have forgotten about her by now, but memories of that night kept playing over and over in his mind.

Audrey's stomping brought him back to the moment. She marched away from the paddock, into the late-afternoon sunshine and kept on going, breezing by him like he wasn't even there. "Fine, Luke. Just fine."

"Don't go getting your spurs in a tangle," he said, following behind.

Her hands flew up and waved in the air and the hat on her head released a few more golden tendrils of hair as she pounded the earth to get away from him. "Just go on your date, Luke. Have fun," she spat out.

She was pissed. She felt that he wouldn't let her do her job. On some level he got that. But he had to watch out for her. There was no sense trying to reason with her right now. Audrey's mind was made up. He was beginning to sympathize with Casey a little bit more. It wasn't easy being responsible for someone else.

Audrey threw up in the toilet bowl. The queasiness came on suddenly when she walked into her bedroom. She had just enough time to make it to the bathroom. "Mercy." She leaned against the wall afterward, holding her pulsating stomach and waiting for it to settle. Thankfully, the slight tremors ebbed after a few minutes and she tossed off her clothes to step into the shower.

She wasn't prone to upsets like this. She'd always had a cast-iron stomach. Casey said she took after their dad. He could eat ice cream and pizza in the morning without any rebellion.

The warming rain of the water eased her agitated nerves. Her body had shaken so badly after her fight with Luke that she'd felt the effects way down in her belly. It had throbbed with anger and frustration. He'd treated her like a child today. He didn't give her the trust she'd needed. He'd been stubborn and bossy, just like Casey. She didn't want to trade one demanding overseer for another. What was the point in that?

And then he'd thrown the final punch to her gut. Katherine.

The thought of Luke with Kat Grady had made her stomach ache. She couldn't hide it, so she'd made a mad dash out of the barn. Thankfully, he'd let her go and hadn't questioned her.

Her stomach seemed fine now, but her heart was another matter. She couldn't bank her jealousy. It was crazy. She hadn't seen Luke for years. He'd probably had dozens of girlfriends, gone on hundreds of dates since his rodeo days.

But you're here now...and have to witness it.

Audrey threw herself into unpacking the boxes from Susanna that had arrived today.

As she lifted one item after another, her tummy was soothed at seeing her familiar things. She put away a few pairs of delicately worn jeans, some blouses, her favorite white cotton undies and bra, a framed picture of Susanna and her in high school and another of Casey and Luke with her as a very young girl standing between them. Then she came to the only photo she had of her mother and father, which was laminated and wrapped in a plastic bag for protection. It was wallet-size and tearing at the edges. The picture always made Audrey long for something that was long since gone—a true family. She hugged the photo to her chest and closed her eyes. The pain of their loss was never far from her mind.

She put that picture in her underwear drawer, on the top and to the side, to keep it from getting crumpled, and then set the other frames atop the dresser, one on each end.

Susanna was a good friend. She knew what Audrey needed.

She'd also sent along Jewel's favorite water bowl and feeding dish along with kitty treats and cat toys. "You are good to go now," she said, tossing Jewel a mouse squeak toy that was three-quarters demolished. The cat gave it a swat and then took a chew, fully occupied and purring.

Audrey wouldn't dwell on where Luke was tonight. She skipped her own dinner entirely. Her stomach needed a rest and she didn't trust herself to eat. But her mouth felt dry and her body needed hydration so she took a stroll to the kitchen.

The house was eerily quiet and dark. She flipped on the lights and poured herself a glass of lemonade. And as she sipped the drink, she wandered over to the oak double French doors and gazed out. The moon was in full force, round and shining like a night beacon, streaming light onto the Slade pool. The glistening waters, so still, so tranquil, reflected back with a twinkle of invitation.

"Not tonight," she mumbled. She finished her drink and padded back to her room. Slipping easily into her T-shirt, she sank into the cozy comfort of the bed. She stroked Jewel behind the ear with one hand and clicked on the TV remote control with the other. This was what her life had turned out to be. In bed early, sitting next to her cat and watching TV.

Her phone barked. "Ruff, ruff." Incoming text. It was probably Susanna wanting to know if the box had arrived safely. Grateful for the interruption, she grabbed her phone and read the text message slicing across the screen.

Are you awake?

It was Luke. She glanced at the clock. Nine-thirty. Her heart sped. Was he home this early? She hadn't heard him come in.

Yes. Hot date over already?

There was a long pause before the next message came through.

Nothing hot about it.

You have my sympathy.

Not really. Inside, she was doing backflips.

Are you home?

Sitting out back. Beautiful night.

I know.

Want to join me?

Yes. Yes. Yes. She held her breath and typed.

I'm still mad at you.

I have beer.

Her stomach couldn't handle alcohol.

Will I get an apology?

Another long pause. Audrey may have pushed her luck. She wanted to see Luke, but it couldn't always be on his terms. She had to stand her ground. She was hired to do a job here and Luke was being bullheaded.

Maybe. Could use some company.

The *maybe* was promising, but it was the last part of the text that broke down her anger and ripped into her heart.

Luke needed a friend. He might have had a tough night tonight, for all she knew. After all, he'd come home early. He needed someone to talk to. How could she refuse him that?

She jumped from the bed and donned her clothes, typing in the words that secured her a seat next to him.

I'll be right there.

She sat on a pool chair facing the water and the great pastures beyond. Luke sat next to her, sipping beer. For a while, they just sat there quietly, Luke deep in his own thoughts. It was nice knowing he felt comfortable enough with her not to have to make small talk. There was a connection between them that felt right.

After a while, Luke toyed with the bottle he'd just drained, palming it from one hand to the other. "You know," he began, "I've been thinking that I've been a little hard on you."

Audrey sat still, her breath stuck in her throat.

"You know your way around horses and I have to trust in that. It's just that I'm used to worrying over you, and Casey would hang my hide if anything happened to you on my watch. Trib is a perplexing case. He's hard to break and he doesn't trust anyone. I found that out the hard way and I don't want a repeat of my mistake happening to you."

Audrey put resolution in her quiet words. "I understand your concern. But, if anything happened to me, it wouldn't be your fault. I take full responsibility for my actions. You don't have to protect me."

His eyes narrowed and he ran a hand back and forth over his forehead. "I know that, I guess."

"Are you sorry you hired me?"

He gave her a quick, guilty look and took a long time to answer. "No."

She didn't quite believe him. "Then let me do my job."

He began nodding slowly. "Okay, okay. But I want a daily report about your progress."

"Meaning you want to check up on me."

He grinned and then defended his reasoning. "You're like my kid sister."

"I'm not a *kid.* And I'm not your *sister.*"

There was force behind her words, and Luke blinked at her tone and then stared at her. "I guess I'm striking out with females today."

Audrey let her frustration drop. She was curious about his date and took that as an opening to bring up the subject. "You had a lukewarm date with good old Katherine?"

Luke focused his gaze on the pasture. He wouldn't look at her. "I broke it off."

She'd been ready to do more mental backflips, but Luke sounded too miserable for her to start celebrating. "What happened?"

He shrugged. "It was never much of anything. We're friendly. We talked tonight and I figured it was best to lay it on the line. It's not in me to pretend something I don't feel. She's nice and all, but something is off…. Can't figure out what that is. And it's serious stuff when a baby is involved. I think mostly she's lonely and a little worried. She's caring for the baby's great-aunt and her health isn't so good."

"How did she take you breaking it off?"

"She said she understood, but I feel like a heel."

"You did the right thing, Luke."

He gave his head a shake. "I couldn't walk in there and pretend to feel something for her I didn't feel. I don't plan on making the same mistakes my folks made."

"Your parents didn't love each other?"

"They did in their own way. But it wasn't the kind of love you build on. There were business reasons for the marriage and then Logan came along and they stuck it out. But my father wasn't happy and when he found the woman who could make him happy, he had to let her go. I think he died regretting it."

Audrey's heart ached for both of his parents. It wasn't the way a woman wanted to be loved. And it wasn't the way a man wanted to love. Halfway. Audrey had enough halves in her own life to know she wanted it all.

This was the first time Luke had confided anything so personal to her. He was feeling low and had wanted her company.

As a friend.

She could be that to him any day of the week. She took his hand in hers. They sat there quietly together, comfortable in the silence. "I forgive you, by the way."

Luke smiled. "I didn't apologize."

"Yes, you did. You just don't know it yet."

Audrey had promised Luke she'd be extremely careful working with Trib today. He was off for an day-long business trip to Vegas this morning and she'd seen the concern on his face and question in his eyes before he left. Giving her the freedom she needed troubled him. He felt such responsibility. That was the reason that she hadn't spilled the truth last night. They'd been alone and sharing confidences by the pool. It would have been the perfect time, if Luke hadn't been feeling down. But her news would have sent him over the edge.

At least that's what she told herself.

Dressed and ready for a full day, Audrey waved to Hunter as she made her way into the barn. "Good morning," she said.

"Hi, Audrey. I've got Felicia, Starlight and Melody already turned out in the corral. You want to exercise Belle and Buck and I'll get the others?"

"Sure. I'll do it before it gets too hot for them. You want to ride together this morning?"

"We could do that, surely."

Audrey liked Hunter. He was genuine and good-natured if not a little bit shy. During their rides she got a chance to know him a little better. They had one thing in common, their love of horses. He'd been practically raised on Sunset Ranch; Ward Halliday, his father, had been the head wrangler here for over twenty years. Ward had been a good friend to Randall Slade and every so often Hunter would recite a story from back in the day. The Slade boys weren't angels in their youth and Audrey loved hearing tales of their antics.

After the morning ride, she spent the better part of the day washing down and grooming the horses. Every few hours, she would pay a visit to Trib. She let him see her. She wanted him to know she was there and would be returning time and again. She wanted him to become familiar with her.

"I'm here and I'm coming back soon. Don't you worry," she'd say.

The horse didn't respond, except to look at her with cautious eyes.

Other than Luke, Ward was the only hand allowed to turn him out to his special corral. One day soon, Audrey would do that. She would also ride him.

For now, each time she was about to exit the paddock, she would leave something special for the stallion on the ground. A few sugar cubes. A scoop of oats. A carrot.

She'd walk out of the barn and into the hot Nevada sunshine, putting her ear to the barn door. She'd listen and, after a few minutes, hear Trib wander over and gobble up his treat.

At the end of the day, Audrey entered the Slade home feeling a sense of accomplishment. She hummed through her shower and dressed in her new clothes, leaving her long blond hair down for a change.

Sophia had invited her to the cottage when she found out Luke would be gone for the day. But Audrey suspected Luke had something to do with that invitation. She didn't mind. She liked spending time with Sophia and Logan. The two were a testament to true love.

Dinner was lovely. Sophia was a gracious host. Logan

grilled steaks outside and Sophia and Audrey made side dishes to complement the meal. Afterward, Logan took a rare long-distance phone call from his brother Justin, who was on his last tour of duty in Afghanistan and due to come home soon. The phone call gave her some private time to spend with Sophia.

Sophia was easy to be around. She didn't judge. She was a good listener and Audrey opened up to her about her life on the road with Casey. About her dreams of becoming a veterinarian and how Casey's injury had slowed that down. Sophia encouraged her to pursue her dreams, as long as she was sure of what she truly wanted.

Audrey left the cottage at nine o'clock after thanking the Slades for a wonderful evening. She parked her truck and headed toward the house. The ranch was quietly settled for the night, the sky starless and black, the air heavy with the day's lingering heat. Not even an owl hooted. The horses were sleeping. Only Jewel greeted her at the door, rubbing against her leg and purring as Audrey walked inside. She wasn't entirely alone; the cat was here. As much as she loved Jewel, somehow that wasn't enough. Seeing Logan and Sophia tonight being so much in love and truly in tune with each other left her feeling a little lost.

It was strange. She was happy for them, but pangs of sadness hit her as she walked into the home of the man she loved. Luke wasn't here. She wanted to talk to him. She'd promised to give him a daily update of her work with Trib. She wanted to share with him the little progress she'd made. But more so, she wanted his company. She missed him and didn't want to waste another second of her time here at Sunset Ranch. Sensations of loneliness rippled over her that far outweighed being physically alone in this big house. She felt it deep in her bones and an unwelcome shiver crept up her spine. Sleep wasn't going to happen right now. And she was too darn edgy for mindless television. She needed a lift, a boost to get her out of this peculiar mood.

An idea struck and her lips curled up.

A skinny-dip was out of the question.

But she did have one other option.

Luke texted Audrey on his way home from the airport. She didn't answer. He glanced at his watch. It was after ten. By all rights she should be in bed by now. Everyone who worked the ranch woke at dawn, put in their hours and it was lights-out by nine usually. She must be asleep after having had dinner at the cottage. But he hadn't heard from her today. He knew darn well she'd jump at the chance to work with Trib. It was a hard call for him to make, giving her that freedom, especially when he wasn't going to be around. He'd worried over it at odd times today but gave Audrey credit for being smart with animals. She'd pretty much insisted on it. He hoped like hell nothing had gone wrong.

His mind flashed to the jet-black stallion rearing up on hind legs and stomping down on his body.

He scrubbed his jaw with his free hand and blew out a deep breath as he drove his truck past the ranch gates. He'd never forget the chest-crushing agony he'd endured when the two hooves beat down on him. Luckily, his body had curled up in a defensive position and rolled partway away. The brunt of Trib's horsepower hadn't hit him, or he probably wouldn't be here today.

He bounded from the truck and strode into the house. Nothing stirred. The house was empty but for one wisp of a girl sleeping in her room. Luke strode to the parlor and poured himself a shot of Jim Beam. He sipped his drink and headed to the kitchen to grab a late-night snack. Maybe Sophia had sent Audrey home with leftovers. He could only hope.

A distant sound filtered through an opened inch of the kitchen window. Luke gathered his brows. It sounded like a splash. He strode to the sliding door and gazed out. Only a slice of the moon appeared, not enough to brighten the sky, but lamps by the water's edge illuminated a female figure in the pool. Luke opened the door without making a sound and stepped outside.

His eyes adjusted to the dim light. The figure of a woman in a red thong bikini emerged clearly now. Her back was to him, her feet skimming the shallow steps of the pool. He zeroed in on her derriere and the sliver of cherry material pressed between twin cheeks of firm melon-shaped eye-popping perfection.

A fast flash of recollection jolted through his system, a dropkick of reality. That murky mystifying night at the cabin was beginning to clear. *He knew that body.*

He swallowed silently and shifted his gaze, hoping to find he'd been mistaken. Hoping to hell it was a wicked trick of the eyes. His gaze locked onto coltish and beautifully sculpted legs, glistening with droplets of water.

He shook his head in denial. *It couldn't be.*

But dread knocked into his gut.

He forced his gaze to travel upward, to the flowing blond waves cascading down the woman's back in layers of un-restrained freedom. His body seized up in a viselike grip. Choked with the truth, he couldn't breathe. Flashes of memory brightened, shining revealing light on the mystery.

Those golden locks of hair had tickled his chin.

Those smooth shapely legs had straddled his body.

Those arousing perfect cheeks had caressed his thighs.

His boots ate up the distance to the pool's edge.

She sensed his presence and whirled around to face him.

"It was you." He heard the disbelief rolling off his tongue.

Her eyes widened with fear. She must've thought he was a stranger, but the second she recognized him coming out of the shadows, her expression quickly changed to guilt.

He caught her red-handed and there was no denying it.

"Luke, I…"

"It was you all along," he repeated. "That night in the cabin."

Luke had never really been aware of the grown-up, feminine version of Audrey before. But now, he couldn't help noticing. She was a stunner in that strip-of-nothing swimsuit. There wasn't much more material on the front side of her suit than there was on the back. Her breasts filled and then spilled out of the top. She was every man's fantasy, a freaking advertisement for sexy and untouchable. Except that he had touched her. He'd touched every inch of her body.

The shock of it bore down on him like a two-thousand-pound steer. He was torn between anger at her deception and raw, unequalled lust. How the hell hadn't he figured this out before now? Was it that her work clothes had concealed an hourglass figure that could send a man straight to heaven… or hell, in his case? Or was it that the idea of making love to Audrey would've never crossed his mind? Or was it that he'd shoved the memory of the seduction to the hidden recesses of his mind because *she* wasn't an option?

All three reasons held merit.

"I'm glad you remember now." The bravado in her soft voice stilled his heart.

"That night, you came into my room—"

"My room," she corrected.

"You came to me without hesitation."

She'd climbed into the bed with bold intentions. Luke had taken what she'd offered—a woman who hadn't been shy about what she wanted.

Audrey took one step up from the shallow end of the pool. The scent of Sweet and Wicked drifted to his nose. Beads of water caressed her body. Lamps beat down and glowed over her beautiful, soft skin. He itched to touch her, to untie the top of her suit and fill his hands with the spillage. A tremor of need ran through him.

"You called me over to the bed."

"I didn't know it was you, darlin'."

"I didn't know that," she whispered. "I thought you knew who I was." The softness of her words traveled over his skin.

From what he did remember, she'd pretty much rocked his world that night. In the morning, he'd woken up sated and smiling and ready for round two, but his mystery woman was gone. He was left to wonder who she was. She'd plagued his thoughts ever since.

The whole thing was beyond wrong.

"It was a mistake. It shouldn't have happened," he told her.

"It wasn't a mistake." Her quiet defiance lifted her chin. "It wasn't planned, but it wasn't a mistake."

"Audrey Faith. Look, I know you had a bad breakup and that you weren't yourself that nigh—"

"I'm not Audrey Faith anymore, Luke. I'm Audrey. I'm an adult and I knew exactly what I was doing when I climbed into your bed and made love to you."

Luke squeezed his eyes shut and drew oxygen into his lungs. Hearing her admit to seducing him got his juices flowing. He was turned on, big-time. Not his proudest moment, but he couldn't force his memory to shut down. For weeks he hoped to hell he'd remember. Now, those flashbacks wouldn't go away. She'd been stark naked and straddling him in the dark, her hair whipping about her face in a frenzy, the scent on her lips and her soft skin driving him wild.

She stood on the second step of the pool, a mass of long, golden hair tumbling past her shoulders, her soft dewy skin moist and glimmering under the lamplight. Her eyes were big and round, the expression on her face fragile enough for him to choose his words carefully. "Audrey—"

"Do you know what it does to a woman not to have a man remember her?"

His throat worked and he swallowed hard, recognizing the injury in her voice. He did remember the act, just not the woman performing the act. He knew that wouldn't make her feel any better. Luke stumbled through his next thoughts. The whole Audrey package made him a little dizzy. And a whole lot of nervous.

He should be angry at her for showing up on the ranch and not telling him the truth immediately. He should be scolding her for letting it go this long, for having sex with him without protection. How the hell did she know that he hadn't been sleeping around? And why had she run off in the morning without a word? Now that was an argument he could sink his teeth into.

But he didn't want to fight with her. He didn't want to scold her like a child. Clearly, she wasn't one. That had become obvious the second he spotted her in the pool. She'd hidden her beauty under scratchy straw hats and youthful ponytails and baggy clothes.

Luke viewed her differently now. But that wouldn't serve him too well. He was mentally knocking himself upside the head. Because she tempted him like no other woman had. She was clearly off-limits, but he couldn't stop the memories from bouncing around his feverish mind. Or put a halt to nerves that were stretched thin by his physical reaction to her.

Now he had the correct face to go with the memory of that night.

And the newfound recollection was worse than the mystery.

The hell of it was, he would never forget making love to Casey's sister, a woman he had always tried to protect.

"I was drugged up and not thinking clear. But you," he began, pointing his finger, looking deep into her wide, expectant eyes, "you should've…" But he couldn't follow through on his reprimand. He dropped his hand suddenly. Hell, he wasn't her teacher or her brother. He took another gulp of air before admitting…he was her lover.

"I should've what?" she asked with a hushed breath.

Luke flicked his gaze over her curvy body. That red thong was messing with his head. He was a man first and foremost and Audrey was killing him in small doses.

He shook his head. "Nothing."

Audrey stepped out of the water, coming up from the last step to plant her feet on solid ground. Even her toes were pretty and now the physical barrier between them was gone. "Nothing?"

Luke didn't respond. Anything he said would either hurt her or get him into trouble. It was the rock *and* the hard place.

"I'm going to bed," he said. It was a good way of settling the matter. In the morning, they'd see things more clearly and could have a serious conversation about it over breakfast.

He had every intention of pivoting on his boot heels and hightailing it inside the house, but his legs weren't moving. He stood rooted to the spot, just a few feet away from the woman clad in a smoking-hot bikini. He needed perspective. He needed to get away, but his brain worked in conjunction with his feet now and nothing budged.

Except Audrey.

She took a step closer and faced him from inches away, the lamps shining a golden halolike glow around her head. His reluctance to move parted her sweet lips and her eyes darkened to a seductive shade. "You don't want to leave."

Slowly, she reached behind herself and grabbed the ties of her halter top at the back of her neck. Fascinated and overwrought with desire, Luke couldn't utter a word. He couldn't tell her to stop. He couldn't tell her this was crazy. She was his mystery woman and he'd secretly hoped to have a thrilling repeat of the night they'd shared.

He could only watch, his body singing a lusty tune, as she gave a slight tug. The material fell away and two beautifully round breasts bounced free on her chest. Shadowy light touched upon ripe pink-hued nipples that lifted toward the sky. His groin tightened at her perfection and the memory of weighing her in his hands, tasting her with his tongue.

"I ran away from you once, Luke. That won't happen again."

Five

Luke wasn't a weak man but he wasn't a damn saint, either. And Audrey was a temptation he couldn't resist tonight. She was naked but for the strip of material below her navel. One flick of his finger and she'd be fully bared to him. Being with the blonde mystery woman again was his fantasy come true.

On impulse, Luke reached for Audrey, wrapping his arms around her slender waist. He gave a sharp tug and she landed up against him, soaking his shirt with her wet skin, her breasts pressed to his chest. Her arms automatically circled his neck and he breathed in Sweet and Wicked again. With his thumb, he shoved her chin up. He bent his head and crushed her mouth with a kiss. A long, deep whimper rose from her throat and he groaned from the depths of his chest, drowning out her sexy sounds of passion.

The kiss wasn't sweet or patient. He demanded that she meet him on his turf. Audrey had no trouble keeping up. Not even when his tongue shoved through her lips and found hers. He swept inside the hollows of her mouth, drawing her out with full strokes that had her body rocking against his in a rhythm that seized his soul and wouldn't let go.

There was no end in sight. He couldn't fathom putting a halt to this. He was consumed now with Audrey's heady, willing and pliant body. She was his for the taking and Luke blocked out any thoughts that said otherwise.

He ran his hands through her hair, weaving his fingers through the silky strands as he kissed her. Leaning her back, he left her mouth to drizzle kisses on the tip of her chin and along her neck, then went farther south to nip at the base of her throat. One hand left her hair to cup her breast. He squeezed gently and filled his palm with a different kind of softness, rounded and silky smooth. His thumb flicked her nipple back and forth.

She moaned and Luke's erection battled against the constraints of his pants. "So beautiful," he muttered, barely able to breathe.

He rubbed his chin over her other breast, teasing the nipple right before he drew it deep into his mouth. He suckled her and stroked the nub with his tongue, until her breathing came in short, labored bursts. "Luke."

Her plea tore at his willpower. He was lost. He'd had her once before, but this time was different. This time they both knew the score. There might be hell to pay later, but Luke was in the now and nothing was going to stop him from taking his mystery woman the way he'd dreamed so many times in the past. "I'm not gonna slow down, honey."

"I…don't…want you to," she eeked out.

Audrey's hands threaded through his hair and she hung on as he worked her into a frenzied state. He wasn't far behind. His blood pulsed through his veins.

He gave her a short, quick kiss then cupped her bottom in both of his palms and lifted her. He loved how she responded to him, without question or qualm. Her legs wrapped around his waist easily and he moved her to the cushioned lounge

chair. Her butt was firm and silky smooth and before he lowered her down, he gave her a squeeze, filling his hands. His
manhood responded and he almost lost it then. Somehow he
managed to regain control and lowered her down.

She gazed up at him, her eyes bright and glazed with passion. In the lamplight, she was amazing and all his. Luke
threw caution to the wind, no matter the warning bells going
off in the furthest reaches of his mind.

"Take off your shirt, Luke." Her plea, and the picture she
made on that cushiony lounge, made his mouth go dry. Her
lips were swollen. Golden hair curled around and framed her
beautiful breasts. Her legs were long and sleek. Every inch of
her body was poised and ready for him. "I want to touch you."

His shirt was gone in an instant and he sat on the edge of
the lounge, letting Audrey's hands roam over his chest. His
skin flamed from her touch. She rose up and kissed him on
the mouth, then lowered her head to kiss the parts of his body
exposed to her.

He could only take so much. He kissed her while gently
shoving her back against the lounge and then did the thing
he'd imagined doing when he'd first seen her wading in the
pool. He hooked his finger into her bikini bottom and slowly,
carefully eased it down her legs.

Even then, Audrey wasn't shy with him. She gave him a
satisfied smile and reached for him again. White-hot heat
swamped his body. But this time he was in control. This time,
he would bring her pleasure.

They were alone in the dark. The night was silent. Neigh-
boring ranches were miles away and Luke's pool area was
private and fenced off in the backyard. Barn scents on the
property blew by on occasional breezes, a familiar and welcome smell of horses and leather.

He ran his fingers along the inner smoothness of her thighs
until he came to the apex of her legs. She lifted her hips up,
parted her lips and closed her eyes, ready for whatever he

would do to her. She trusted him without pause. Luke valued that trust and began to stroke her, slow and easy, teasing her with light touches. "Do you like that?"

She swallowed and nodded. "Yes."

"I thought you would. Tell me when you want more."

"I want more," she whispered, and Luke grinned.

He slid two fingers over her again, slipping them inside this time and gliding them back and forth, inside and out. "Oh," she moaned.

The throaty sounds she made burned clear through him. He stretched out beside her on the lounge and kissed her in keeping with his fingers' steady cadence. She squirmed with need and Luke sped up his pace, touching her in ways that would only give her the most satisfaction.

When her release came, Luke wasn't ready for the long, drawn-out sighs of contentment that whispered from her lips.

Wrapped in his shirt, Audrey reclined on Luke's bed after he deposited her there with utmost care. No words had been spoken on the way to his room. With eyes locked on each other and refusing to break the connection, they were in silent agreement. Luke had just made her world spin out of control. She was happier than she'd ever been in her life.

"Are you sure about this?" Luke came down on the bed beside her, trailing kisses along her jawline.

She nodded, too overwhelmed to speak at the moment.

She wove her hands in his hair as he continued to kiss her. She felt his need breaking through the restraint he'd managed as he'd scooped her up into his arms from the lounge chair to bring her inside.

Just a glimmer of light came through the walnut-wood shutters. The bed was big and comfortable, and she didn't care where she ended up, as long as Luke was beside her.

He took his time with her, kissing her gently, stroking her

body tenderly and speaking soft words in her ear. The evidence of his desire pressed the side of her body.

She slid her hand onto his chest, feeling hot, firm skin and powerful muscles underneath her fingertips. Fanning her fingers across washboard abs, she let go a sigh. How many times had she dreamed of this? How many times had she wished she would once again have the freedom to touch Luke and feel his body come alive with hers?

She reached for his belt buckle, helping him unfasten it. Boots flew and pants were tossed aside quickly after that. Audrey got a glimpse of Luke approaching her and her breath caught in her throat. His hair was pushed back and sandy tendrils curled at his shoulders. His chest was big and broad and when she darted a glance lower, her memory was jolted back to weeks before, and how she'd enjoyed every fulfilling second of their lovemaking.

"Come closer, Luke," she said, repeating the words he'd whispered in the cabin.

He stood tall by the side of the bed like a Greek god, tanned and mighty.

She watched him sheath his manhood and then slide a lingering glance over her entire body. Warm waves of expectation zinged through her belly. Before he climbed onto the bed, he cupped her womanhood and stroked her with the heel of his hand several times, making her mind go fuzzy and her heartbeats speed up. Everything inside turned to hot jelly.

He took her thighs in his hands and spread them, then lowered himself over her. Her eyes were wide with wonder. She didn't want to miss any part of this. She needed Luke and wanted to see him take pleasure from her body, in much the same way he had given to her. With a potent thrust, he filled her and closed his eyes. "So tight," he said with a deep rasp. "So good."

He moved on her slowly and she followed his lead, her heart swelling with love. She gave back to him thrust for thrust, and when he increased the pressure and rose above her, she bowed her body back to accommodate him. He took her hips in his hands and drove harder, faster, bending her back even more. Then she closed her eyes and her body burst into flames when he pressed his thumb where they were joined. It was only seconds later that everything spun crazily out of control. Her breaths were short, quick puffs and her body seized up just as Luke let out a long satisfied groan from the depths of his chest. Their cries mingled in the still night and echoed against the walls in a chorus of sweeping sensual sounds.

Every drop of strength oozed from her limbs. She couldn't move, yet she was floating. And Luke, the maker of dreams, was slow to remove himself from her body. He held on and watched her come gracefully down to earth. He took a swallow and bent to kiss her on the lips before he slid to the side of the bed.

He entwined their fingers and set them on his chest. "Are you okay?" he asked, staring at the ceiling.

She was in heaven. "I'm fine."

His gaze roamed over her naked body, taking a leisurely tour. "I'll be agreeing with you there. You're fine."

She smiled at his compliment. After all the years of yearning, wanting and loving Luke, she could finally savor and enjoy this moment. Beams of happiness set her heart aglow. She was where she'd always wanted to be.

"Are you cold?" Gripping the sheet, he was ready to cover her.

"Not at all."

He let the sheet drop and kissed her shoulder, and another wave of warmth coursed through her body. She'd never be cold with Luke nearby. He was beautiful, a perfectly muscled man of the earth. A modern-day cowboy who loved the same things she did.

He leaned back against the bed, staring up at the ceiling

again. He seemed to go someplace that put a frown on his face and then his jaw twitched as if in pain. It only took a minute for his demeanor to change. A long sigh, heavy with regret, rose from his chest.

Audrey prayed she was imagining his change in mood. She wasn't ready for a lecture right now. She wanted to bask in the glory of their lovemaking.

"Why'd you do it, Audrey?" he asked.

She squeezed her eyes closed. "Do what?" But she knew.

"Why'd you come to me that night in the cabin?"

Because I've loved you for the past ten years. Dare she tell him? What if he had the same feelings for her and was only just discovering them now? "I was ready to be impulsive."

"So it was payback. You caught your boyfriend cheating and wanted to get back at him?"

"More like, I didn't care that I'd caught him cheating. It bummed me out to know that I'd invested that much time in a guy I didn't care about."

"Wow. That's deep but I get it."

"You do?" Now that was a revelation. Usually when a girl went philosophical on a guy, he shut down completely. But this was classic Luke. He was easy to talk to and he understood her.

"Yeah, I do. And I get why you ran off that night. You realized your lapse in judgment and couldn't face me in the morning. We're friends, Audrey. But I hadn't seen you in years."

Audrey covered herself with the sheet and hinged up into a sitting position. "It wasn't a lapse of any kind, Luke. That's not why I ran off."

"Then why? Was it because of Casey? Were you afraid of his reaction?"

Luke's expression grew grim. His brows lifted and his eyes widened as if he'd just remembered that Casey was her brother. "Ah, hell. *Casey.*" He winced. "Your brother trusted me to watch out for you and twice now I've betrayed that trust."

"That's not true. You didn't betray anyone."

"Casey warned me you were vulnerable and hurt. And what do I do? The first chance I get, I sleep with his sister."

"I'm not just Casey's sister, Luke. I'm a grown woman capable of making my own decisions."

"I take one look at you in that pool and I can't resist. What does that say about me?"

"You're a man? And maybe you like me a little?"

He twisted his face and blew air out of his lungs.

"Casey had no right interfering in this or telling you about my personal problems," Audrey said. "He surely didn't know I was coming here."

"Yeah, about that…" Luke bounded off the bed and looked around the floor for his boxers. Once found, he put them on and moved to turn on a dimmer light switch. The room was suddenly bathed in a soft glow. He stood by the bed with his hands on his hips now. She'd seen that dubious expression on his face before. He was in interrogation mode. Still gorgeous, still hunky, but with a rigid set to his jaw. "If you weren't coming here for a job, then why'd you show up on the ranch? I want the truth this time."

"I always tell you the truth, Luke."

"I had no idea we slept together, Audrey. You ran off and left me to wonder about a mystery woman."

"Do you always go to bed with women you don't know?" That question had kept her up at night. If he hadn't known it was her, who did he think he was making love to?

His head jerked back. Surprise registered on his face. She'd turned the tables on him and he didn't much like it. "I thought I knew who it was. *Obviously.*"

"Obviously. So who?"

"A woman I'd seen that night at the party. A blonde."

Jealousy burned in her heart. "But not someone you knew very well."

Luke looked away, unable to meet her gaze. "I wasn't... thinking clearly."

"But you were tonight."

He turned to face her, his eyes filled with guilt and regret. That anguished look seared into her every pore.

Don't, Luke. Don't you dare regret this.

Mentally, Audrey spun the Worst-Case Scenario game wheel and wondered where it would land. Was it worse that Luke didn't know he'd made love to her the first time, or that he regretted it down to his toes the second time? Either way, she came out the loser.

He nodded, looking none too happy with himself.

She wanted to go back to ten minutes ago, when life was beautiful.

Now, looking at the pain on Luke's face, all she felt was heartache.

"Answer my question, Audrey. Why did you show up here?"

"I came to own up to running out on you. I felt bad. I didn't know if you were mad at me, or relieved that I had disappeared from your life. I came to Sunset Ranch to discuss that night with you. But when I realized you didn't know it was me in that bedroom, I lost my nerve. It's a pretty low blow to have a man not know he made love to you. Especially since it meant so much to me."

"It meant so much to..." Luke didn't finish the sentence. He was too busy twisting his lips and squeezing his eyes closed in disbelief. He began shaking his head. "Don't go there, Audrey."

He found his jeans and put them on, zipping them up with a quick pull. "We had a good time tonight." He tempered his voice as if afraid to bruise her ego. As if he was speaking to a child. "But don't go reading anything else into this. If you hadn't seduced me in the first place we wouldn't be in this mess."

"You're blaming me for seducing you after what we just shared in this bedroom?"

He continued to shake his head. "When I saw you in the pool, everything clicked into place. I was surprised by you and the temptation to re-create something that's been haunting me took over."

"We did re-create it. It was even better than the first time."

Another heavy sigh escaped. "I'm going to my grave regretting what just happened."

His words slapped across her face. Her cheeks burned with pain. She'd given herself to him again, this time in the hopes of starting something new between them. Something more than friendship, but Luke didn't see it that way. He saw it as a *mess*. He couldn't see beyond the girl she used to be to the woman she was today. And Mr. Nice Guy had guilt because of a promise he'd made to Casey. It hurt like hell and wasn't fair.

Audrey couldn't stay in his room tonight. She couldn't stand to see Luke try to make amends for making love to her or speak about his regret again. That would be the last straw.

She yanked the sheet from the bed and wrapped it around her body then stood up to face him. Her pride bruised, she hid her injury and the pain his words inflicted. "You don't have to regret anything, Luke. Consider it forgotten. A mistake, like you said. A big fat lapse in judgment. You don't have to tell me more than once. I get it."

She held her grief inside, hoisted her chin and marched to the door. Then she whirled around, opened her hand and let the expensive Egyptian cotton sheet fall gracefully to the floor. Buck naked, she had Luke's full attention. His eyes flickered over her body. A few seconds ticked by. Then she turned her back on him. "I'll see you at breakfast," she tossed over her shoulder as she walked out the door.

* * *

The next five breakfasts were quiet affairs. For the most part, Audrey wasn't speaking to Luke except for matters that regarded the ranch. She was invested here now with the animals, especially Trib, and she'd vowed to never again run away because things got tough, so thoughts of leaving the ranch—and Luke—skipped right out of her head.

She spent her days with Hunter and Ward and met with Sophia for lunch several times. She poured herself into the work, adding additional chores to her regimen to keep her mind busy and her heart from sinking into the bowels of the earth. Luke didn't seem all that concerned that their friendship was on stilted terms. He was probably relieved he didn't have to deal with her. He didn't have to pretend to feel something for her that he didn't feel.

It was harder on her. She hadn't breathed a word about what had happened between them to anyone. But every so often, Sophia would bring up Luke's name in conversation and Audrey would shrug a shoulder or give a clipped response. Sophia was smart enough to be a little suspicious, but Audrey managed to change the subject without fanfare or being too obvious.

For the past three afternoons, she'd worked with Trib at the barn. She wouldn't allow her personal feelings to interfere with the job she was hired to do. Luke had come by to watch her progress, keeping a big distance away as she'd asked. But his eagle eyes were on her and she resented that his presence there was solely to make sure she wasn't in danger.

He was always protecting her.

Any other female would've loved the attention. Was she a fool? She ached inside knowing she'd lost Luke as a friend. Though she wanted him as a lover. No, that wasn't true. She wanted to be more than his lover. She wanted a real relationship with him. But she'd have gladly taken more nights like the one they'd shared, hoping it would lead to a richer relationship.

Now Audrey had nothing. No friendship. No lover. No Luke.

Yet, she couldn't bring herself to leave the ranch. She couldn't quit another thing. She was through doing things halfway. She had a job to do; the ranch depended on her, and she felt the challenge of Trib deep down in her bones. Leaving Luke and the ranch would be the easy way out in one respect. She wouldn't have the constant reminder of what she couldn't have. But she would have satisfaction knowing she accomplished something and didn't run at the first sign of trouble.

Luke's painful words rang in her ears; it was a sharp dagger to her heart as she recalled the last thing he'd said to her that night.

I'm going to my grave regretting what just happened.

She didn't want to be anyone's last regret.

Newly fueled anger surged through her system.

The anger did nothing to quell her constant fatigue. Instead, she felt lifeless, her arms and legs weak and her body limping along. She blamed it on Luke. She blamed everything on Luke these days.

After another long day of working with the horses, she came back to the house, peeled off her work clothes and stepped into the shower. A soothing stream of water rained down to refresh her body and her mind. *Wash Luke away from my thoughts tonight,* she implored the water gods. *Heal my heartache and soothe my soul.* Was it too much to ask of a water god? She didn't know but when she wrapped herself into a towel and dried off, she felt a little better.

She was ready for mindless television and a good night's sleep.

She climbed into bed and gave Jewel a big, body-squeezing hug. The cat purred immediately and rubbed her face against her leg. Then she did a belly roll, content in the outpouring of attention she was receiving lately. Audrey accommodated her, petting her under the chin. When the cat rolled over, having had enough undivided attention, Audrey got comfy and picked up the remote control and clicked the TV on.

"Looks like *Wannabes and Wranglers* is on tonight."

It was nice having a cat around to pretend you weren't talking to yourself.

Audrey watched, noting John Wannabe's progress. He rode tall in the saddle now. He actually looked good, but he hadn't mastered the reins just yet...uh-oh. The horse took off at a run. John's hat flew off his head and it was all he could do to stay on the runaway horse...

A dog's bark came from her phone.

Jewel lifted her head again. "It's a text," she said to the cat. Audrey peeked at the screen. It was from Luke.

Are you watching?

Yes,

she messaged back, even though she didn't want to have a conversation with him tonight.

John should hang it up now before he gets seriously hurt.

Maybe John's not a quitter.

It was her anger speaking. She didn't care if Luke read between the lines. One way or another, Audrey would get her point across.

She didn't hear back from Luke until five minutes before the reality show ended.

John got voted off. Probably saved his skin and his neck.

She wrote back,

He was willing to take the hard knocks to achieve his goals. Too bad the others didn't have faith in him. I'm turning in. Good night, Luke.

Audrey shut off the television and sank into the cushy bed. She'd made her point loud and clear and somehow, she didn't feel much like celebrating the slight win. She didn't feel good, period. And the last thing she wanted was to think about Luke right before she fell asleep. She'd probably dream about him.

A soft knock at her bedroom door came thirty seconds after she'd closed her eyes.

It could only be one person.

She could pretend to be asleep. That wouldn't be too far-fetched, would it? But when the second soft knock came, she sighed and tossed off the covers. On bare feet and in her ugly T-shirt that read Cats and Women Know How to Land on Their Feet, she padded to the door.

She wasn't ready for the sight of Luke in faded jeans and a white wifebeater with his arms spread wide, bracing himself against the doorjambs. He leaned in, scruffy day-old beard and all, and she caught the scent of bourbon on his breath. His eyes raked over her legs and followed a path that finally rested on her face. Then his lips tightened to a fine line. "You're in a mood tonight."

She'd been in a mood for several nights. But it was hard concentrating on any of that, with Luke looking like pure sin standing in her bedroom doorway. "Sorry if I disappoint you."

He showed his displeasure by deepening his scowl.

"What do you want?" she asked.

"No argument."

"About what?" Geesh, it was past her bedtime and he was speaking in riddles.

"I'm taking you to Logan and Sophia's engagement party."

A dubious laugh escaped her throat. "Oh, no, you're not."

"Afraid so. Logan asked me specifically and Sophia sec-

Send For
2 FREE BOOKS
Today!

I accept your offer!

Please send me two free
Harlequin® Desire® novels and
two mystery gifts (gifts worth
about $10). I understand that
these books are completely
free—even the shipping and
handling will be paid—and I am
under no obligation to purchase
anything, ever, as explained on the
back of this card.

225/326 HDL FVZ2

Please Print

FIRST NAME

LAST NAME

ADDRESS

APT.#   CITY

STATE/PROV.   ZIP/POSTAL CODE

Visit us online at
www.ReaderService.com

Offer limited to one per household and not applicable to series that subscriber is currently receiving.
Your Privacy—The Harlequin® Reader Service is committed to protecting your privacy. Our Privacy Policy is
available online at www.ReaderService.com or upon request from the Harlequin Reader Service. We make a portion
of our mailing list available to reputable third parties that offer products we believe may interest you. If you prefer that
we not exchange your name with third parties, or if you wish to clarify or modify your communication preferences,
please visit us at www.ReaderService.com/consumerschoice or write to us at Harlequin Reader Service Preference
Service, P.O. Box 9062, Buffalo, NY 14269. Include your complete name and address.

© 2012 HARLEQUIN ENTERPRISES LIMITED. ® and ™ are trademarks owned and used by the trademark owner and/or its licensee. Printed in the U.S.A. ▲ Detach card and mail today. No stamp needed. ▲ HD-RG-06/13

HARLEQUIN READER SERVICE —Here's how it works:

Accepting your 2 free books and 2 free gifts (gifts valued at approximately $10.00) places you under no obligation to buy anything. You may keep the books and gifts and return the shipping statement marked "cancel." If you do not cancel, about a month later we'll send you 6 additional books and bill you just $4.55 each in the U.S. or $4.99 each in Canada. That is a savings of at least 13% off the cover price. It's quite a bargain! Shipping and handling is just 50¢ per book in the U.S. and 75¢ per book in Canada.* You may cancel at any time, but if you choose to continue, every month we'll send you 6 more books, which you may either purchase at the discount price or return to us and cancel your subscription.

*Terms and prices subject to change without notice. Prices do not include applicable taxes. Sales tax applicable in N.Y. Canadian residents will be charged applicable taxes. Offer not valid in Quebec. Credit or debit balances in a customer's account(s) may be offset by any other outstanding balance owed by or to the customer. Please allow 4 to 6 weeks for delivery. Offer available while quantities last. All orders subject to credit approval. Books received may not be as shown.

▼ If offer card is missing write to: Harlequin Reader Service, P.O. Box 1867, Buffalo, NY 14240-1867 or visit www.ReaderService.com ▼

NO POSTAGE
NECESSARY
IF MAILED
IN THE
UNITED STATES

BUSINESS REPLY MAIL
FIRST-CLASS MAIL   PERMIT NO. 717   BUFFALO, NY

POSTAGE WILL BE PAID BY ADDRESSEE

HARLEQUIN READER SERVICE
PO BOX 1867
BUFFALO NY 14240-9952

onded the notion. And you know what that means…there's no arguing that request."

"I can get there on my own, thank you very much."

"Don't be a child, Audrey."

She rolled her shoulders back and stiffened up, which inadvertently jutted her breasts out. Luke's gaze ventured to her chest and a gleam he couldn't hide shined in his eyes.

She rasped, "I think we've already established that I am not a child."

Luke glanced at her hair, which she'd been leaving down lately. Tonight it was wild about her head. Then his gaze lowered to her mouth in a soft caress. If he chose to speak about mistakes or regrets now, the door would fly in his face. "That's been established," he agreed. "But it'll look real suspicious if you and I drive separately. Logan's restaurant, The Hideaway, is up in the hills. It's a windy road and a difficult drive. There's no reason not to carpool."

"Make up an excuse."

"I've already thought of a few. Nothing makes much sense."

She didn't know why that bruised her feelings, since she was the one trying to weasel out of going with him, but it did. He didn't want to take her as much as she didn't want to go with him. But her reason went beyond her anger at him. Going with Luke to a special party for his brother would seem too much like a real dress-up-in-your-fancy-duds kind of date. And for a big part of her life, she had hoped to go on a date with Luke.

"I'll go with Hunter."

"Hunter is driving up with his folks in Ward's truck. There's no room for you. Face it, Audrey. You're stuck with me."

Sort of like being *stuck* with a rock star for the night. Or a prince.

"Fine." She made it clear with that one word that she wasn't too happy about it.

He nodded.

They stared at each other.

Time ticked by.

"You know," he said softly, "it doesn't have to be like this between us."

Yes. It did. She glanced away for a second to compose herself, before turning to look him dead in the eyes. "What did you have in mind?"

She watched his Adam's apple dip down to the base of his throat when he took a swallow. "We can still be friends."

The old let's-be-friends-because-I really-don't-want-to-feel-guilty-anymore ploy. A dozen reasons why she couldn't be Luke's friend right now streamed into her mind. "Sorry, that's not an option."

"Fine." His voice sharp, he didn't conceal his annoyance.

"Fine."

"We'll leave at five on Saturday night."

"I'll be ready. Good night, Luke."

"Uh-huh." He took her in from head to toe one last time, before drawing a deep breath and turning away. She closed the door, slumping her shoulders as righteous anger slowly ebbed from her body. Tears welled in her eyes. Her heart broke a little bit more as she climbed into bed and hugged Jewel tight to her chest, determined not to dream about Luke Slade tonight.

Six

"That dress is made for you," Kat Grady said. The platinum blonde strode from behind the boutique counter to give Audrey a smile. "It's nice to see you again."

"Same here, Kat."

Audrey didn't know what else to do but to give the dress she'd pulled from the rack a studious glance. She'd been flummoxed when she entered the shop to find Kat working here. Apparently, Sophia was just as surprised. Silver Springs was a small town twenty miles west of the ranch, and Sophia had driven her here this afternoon to find a dress appropriate for the engagement party. The boutique was smack in the center of town and from what Audrey gathered, had stylish clothes that she could barely afford. "I promise to stay on my feet this time."

Kat's eyes softened. "Well, I hope you're feeling better."

"Thank you. It was just a little bug," she explained. "I'm fine now." Although lately, she'd been experiencing occasional bouts of fatigue and melancholy.

"I'm glad to hear that. What do you think about the dress?"

Audrey held the sapphire-blue dress an arm's length away from her to admire the Empire waist and silvery jewels that formed a four-inch band underneath the bodice. "It's nice."

"I think it's perfect for you," Sophia said, coming to stand beside her. "The color will draw out your soft complexion. It's a good complement to your skin and blond hair."

"Would you like to try it on?" Kat asked.

"I... Uh, sure."

"Right this way."

"If you don't like the fit, there's a few others I think would be stunning. But let's see how this one looks on you first."

Audrey followed Kat to a good-size dressing room with a three-way mirror. The other woman gently took the dress from her hand to place it on a satin hook. "I hope you like it. Let me know—"

A child's whimpering cry stopped her from finishing the sentence. "Oh, excuse me. That's my son." Kat rushed to the back room that was only steps away from the dressing area.

Audrey watched her go, noting how the woman's entire demeanor changed from cool professional to a woman with worry lines around her mouth.

Audrey slipped out of her clothes and tried on the dress, peering at the fit from all angles in the mirror. Soft material crisscrossed her breasts and draped in pretty folds from the bodice down to her toes. The Empire style suited her body, and seeing herself in such a pretty gown gave her ego the boost it needed. Sophia had been right—the striking sapphire color did bring out the honey-blond of her hair. "Sold," she said to the mirror.

When she redressed in her own clothes and walked back to the sales floor, Kat stood by the counter with a dark-haired baby in her arms. "Shush now, baby. It's okay." She rocked him and the little boy was comforted. "I'm sorry. My son got a little fussy. He woke up from his nap early. Usually he sleeps for two hours in the afternoon."

The little boy, wrapped tight around his mother like a life preserver, and bobbing up and down in her arms, focused his eyes on Audrey. Jet-black hair curled at his nape and chubby cheeks, ruddy now from crying, pressed into his mother's shoulder.

"He's beautiful," Audrey said. "How old?"

Kat continued cradling his head and rocking him. "Connor is nine months. I apologize about this. I'm only filling in for the owner who's having minor surgery today. I promised to keep the shop open, unless Connor prevented it. He's been good for most of the day."

"That's very nice of you." Sophia smiled at the boy. "Do you work here often?"

"Not really. I'd love to, but Connor needs me at home with him."

Audrey's heart warmed. Kat wasn't the blonde bombshell type she'd originally thought her to be. The woman had certainly looked the part though. With highfalutin hair, deep rose-colored lips and stunning clothes, she left an impression. But looks deceived. Seeing her with her child convinced Audrey that she'd been wrong about her. The bond between mother and baby was strong. She beamed when she looked at him. Her voice held motherly pride when she spoke his name. She was a single mother raising a young son all alone.

Audrey understood Luke's reluctance to get involved with Kat now. That adorable baby had to be considered in the mix. Audrey respected Luke for his decision. The man had honor. He wouldn't deliberately hurt anyone for his own selfish needs. Though she wasn't thrilled with Luke lately, she had to give credit where it was due.

Luke had done the right thing with Kat.

With her, he'd been wrong.

"Well, we won't keep you another minute. I love the dress. I'll take it." *And you can close up shop and take your sweet baby home.*

On the way back to the ranch, Audrey stared out of the windshield of Sophia's car. "I guess you can't judge a book by its cover."

"You're talking about Kat?"

Audrey nodded. "Yes, I misjudged her."

"Maybe I did, too."

Audrey tilted her head toward Sophia. "All I saw was a beautiful woman, dressed to the hilt, hanging on Luke's arm, and I assumed I knew the kind of woman she was."

"Don't be so hard on yourself. You let your emotions rule your head. It happens when you're in love," Sophia said softly.

Audrey stiffened in the seat. "I'm not in love." Even to her own ears, her emphatic tone sounded unbelievable. Her shoulders slumped and she lost all of her fight. "Oh…am I that obvious?"

"No, you're not. Except to me. I recognize the signs. It wasn't that long ago that I felt those same love/hate feelings for Logan. There were times I really despised him."

"Luke's such a good guy. Sometimes, I feel guilty for giving him a hard time. But damn it, all of my life, decisions have been taken out of my hands. Luke's still treating me like a kid, telling me what's best for me. Pushing me away for my own good."

"Does he know how you feel about him?"

She shook her head. "No. I mean, I haven't told him. But we've…we've had a night…or two."

Sophia took her eyes off the road to give her a long look. "A night or two? Are you saying…?"

Audrey nodded. She was tired of holding everything inside. Sophia was her friend and she trusted her. She spent the rest of the drive home confessing to Sophia what had happened between her and Luke these past few weeks. Most of it rushed out of her mouth, unpracticed and brutally honest. Sophia asked a few questions here and there but by the time they'd driven through the gates of Sunset Ranch, her friend had gotten the whole picture.

"Wow. That's an amazing story," Sophia said. "Now it's all beginning to make sense."

"I know. I should have told Luke the second I saw him that it was me in the cabin."

"Luke does like honesty."

"He wasn't thrilled with me. We had an argument about it. So do you think I should tell him how I feel?"

Sophia wrinkled her nose and thought about it a second. "Yes, but only when you know the time is right."

"How am I supposed to know that?"

"Well, if he tells you first, that would be a good time." She grinned.

Audrey rolled her eyes. "Like that'll ever happen."

"Don't be so certain it won't. Luke might surprise you."

"I've loved him for so long and now that I'm here living under his roof, I'm no closer to getting what I want than when I was a kid, except I've got a few great memories to take to my grave."

Sophia's eyes warmed with sympathy. She set her hand on her arm. "I'm going to stop by the cottage. I have something you might need, Audrey. I hope you don't think I'm meddling."

"I'd never think that. You've been so good to me since I've been here and I really value your friendship. So what is it? A magic love potion? The key to Luke's heart?"

Sophia's shook her head and didn't laugh at her attempt at levity. "Nothing like that. Luke's my good friend, too, and we're family now. And well, just remember I want what's best for both of you. And again, I hope I'm not out of line here."

"Okay. I'll remember that." Sophia's serious tone made her clamp her mouth shut and wait.

Sophia parked the car in front of the cottage, which was now under renovation to add on several rooms to enlarge the house. "Logan's not home. I'll only be a moment."

When Sophia returned with a small white bag in her hand, she sat in the driver's seat and handed it over to her. "I hope this is…whatever you want it to be." There was joy in her eyes and caution, too. "Open it in the privacy of your bedroom, Audrey."

A shiver rode up and down her spine.

Audrey looked down at the drugstore bag in her lap and knew what it was. The shape of the rectangular box inside removed any doubt she'd had. "I take it this isn't lubricating jelly."

Sophia cracked a smile. "No."

Denial had been her constant companion and now Sophia was making her face the music. Audrey didn't want to think about the possibilities, but the signs—or should she say, symptoms—were all there and Audrey, coward that she was, had done a good job of ignoring them.

"I keep a few on hand. Logan and I have been trying. No one knows that but you now."

Audrey lifted her eyes to Sophia. "Thanks for trusting me with that. I hope it happens."

"It will," Sophia said, a confident glow in her eyes.

She nodded. "You're right, of course. I should find out." She grasped the edges of the bag, rolling them up tight and taking a swallow. "Luke deserves to know the truth."

Sophia leaned over and wrapped her arms around her. She spoke with sincerity. "My concern is for you, Audrey. You need to know the truth. But only when you're ready."

Tears burned behind her eyes. Emotions overwhelmed her. With a lump in her throat and her belly churning, she couldn't get the words out she wanted to say. Finally, she managed, "You're…a…good friend, Sophia."

* * *

That night, Audrey tossed and turned in her bed. The home pregnancy test sat on the bathroom counter, still unopened, still in the bag. She wasn't ready. She didn't know when she'd ever be ready. Her life was one screwed-up mess right now.

Her restless movements annoyed Jewel so much that the cat gave her a sour look, jumped down from the bed and curled up on the captain's chair by the window. "Sorry, Jewel," she said. "You can have the bed back. I'm leaving for a while."

Audrey slipped out of her bed and dressed, tucking her T-shirt into her jeans, putting her boots on and striding out the bedroom door. It was well past midnight and she'd pay for her twitchy sleeplessness in the morning, but right now, she needed to walk and clear her head.

She tiptoed past Luke's room and out of the house, heading for the stables. Where else would she go when she needed comfort? She stopped at the barn that held the prized animals that made up the bulk of Sunset Ranch. Some horses were awake, shuffling around in their stalls. She whispered hellos to them and smiled at the others that were asleep in the prone position, lying on the soft hay and looking so peaceful.

That peace eluded her tonight.

"How's it going, Rusty?" She peered at a reddish-brown gelding making his approach. "You can't sleep, either?" When he hung his head over the stall's door, she gave his silky coat a pat and threaded her fingers through his coarse mane. The textures, smooth against rough, brought a smile to her face. The scent of straw and dung, of earth and dust, comforted her in ways that warmed her heart. "Yeah, we both had a long day, didn't we?" She rubbed her face along his and was awarded with an affectionate nuzzle.

As she passed by the stalls and other horses approached, she gave each one of them attention, but her restlessness didn't fully subside. She was still antsy. Still unsettled. Her feet moved and she kept on walking. Out of that barn, into the dark

and even farther, until she came upon the special building—
the barn where she'd been unconsciously heading all along.

You're tempting fate, Audrey.

Yet she kept taking the strides, kept digging her boot heels
in and moving forward until she reached her final destination
and stared into the coal-black, dangerous eyes of the stallion.

"Hello, Trib."

Beams of sunlight brightened the darkness behind her eyes
and she lifted her lids. Morning dawned and a groan from
deep in her belly emerged to greet the day. She'd only gotten a few hours of sleep. But as tired as she was, her nerves
tingled with excitement when her first thoughts to emerge
were of the stallion she'd visited last night. Trib hadn't been
such a hard case after all. In the solitude of the night, with
darkness surrounding them, Audrey had made headway with
the stallion. It was only slight, but it was headway she could
bank on. The horse had been at loose ends. She could relate.
She'd felt the same way. And in a weird sort of way, she'd
bonded with Trib. He'd come halfway. They'd talked. Well,
she'd talked and the horse had patiently listened. They were
two lost souls, more lonely than anything else. Trib had been
isolated from the animals. He didn't like that, and although he
didn't play well with others among the horse population, how
else would he learn to get along? Audrey had to work with
him, privately and at night, when it was just the two of them.

She would build his trust.

Jewel scratched at the door. The cat was eager to start her
day. She liked the ranch, had free rein to wander the grounds,
annoy the penned-up animals and catch creepy-crawly bugs.

"Okay. I'll let you out."

Audrey tossed her covers off and sat up. Her head spun.
Waves of dizziness hit her. Oh, no. Fainting again wasn't an
option. When it didn't happen, she thanked her lucky stars.
She'd open that drugstore bag soon, but right now, the room

and her head merged onto one axis and she was grateful. She brought deep breaths into her lungs and rose. Steady on her feet now, she took cautious steps to the door to let Jewel out. "Don't get into trouble."

Audrey moved slowly about the room. Just in case. When she was sure she'd remain upright, she showered and dressed. She had a full day of work ahead of her. Weekends knew no free time on a working ranch. Chores still needed doing.

She plopped a hat on her head and hurried down the hallway. Her tummy tender, she opted to bypass the kitchen and skip breakfast this morning. She strode out the front door and headed straight for the barn. She had horses to exercise and groom and she'd promised Ward to look over the feed order, to make sure he hadn't forgotten anything.

She waved at Boyd and Jimmy, two of the hands working in the corral, and bounded inside the barn. She stopped short when she saw Luke in the middle of the barn. He held a besotted Jewel in his arms and was spoiling the cat by scratching her under the chin. Jewel purred loudly. Audrey could swear the cat's mouth curved up into a smile.

"Mornin'," Luke said, walking over.

Heavens. She'd hoped to avoid him today.

"Morning, Luke."

"You missed breakfast. Ellie made bacon, eggs and biscuits."

Her empty stomach jerked at the mention of food. The Slade housekeeper was back. She'd heard she was a great cook. And now her stomach rumbled. "I wasn't hungry." She'd been queasy.

Luke glanced at her old jeans, sloppy blouse and straw hat. She'd been wearing clothes from Sunset Lodge's gift shop but today she'd opted for ultimate comfort rather than style.

"You don't have to work 24/7, Audrey. You already put in your five days."

"I don't consider it work. I enjoy caring for the animals."
She shrugged. "Besides, what else would I do?"

Luke stared at her. His throat worked as his Adam's apple
bobbed up and down. A moment passed between them. Then
he sighed. "Whatever it is women do with their spare time."

"I'm not like most women."

Luke bent to put Jewel down and when he came up, he
was inches from her face. His voice dropped an octave. "I
know, Audrey."

She held her breath. Being near Luke did things to her
equilibrium and she'd already had one bout of dizziness today.
"Then you know I'd rather be with them than anything else."

"Okay," he said, nodding. "But I'm giving the weekend
staff time off in honor of Logan and Sophia's engagement
party. Most of the hands are invited and they could use the
time."

Darn. She'd almost forgotten about the party. She wished
it was any day but today, though. She hadn't started the day
off on a chipper note.

"I haven't gotten daily reports from you about Trib," he
said.

"That's because you've been right there, watching me."

"I can't see a darn thing from where I'm standing and you
know it, Audrey Faith. And if I'm in the area and see you
over there, there's no harm in me being nearby. The horse
doesn't know I'm there."

Audrey wouldn't argue the point. "He's coming around.
I see some progress. He's lonely in there, Luke. I think he
needs company."

"Female company?"

Audrey blushed down to her toes. She wasn't usually prone
to turning five shades of red at the mention of sex, but with
Luke's expression of surprise as if he should've been the
one to think of it, Audrey couldn't keep the color from her
cheeks. "It's not his time, Luke. I meant that he's isolated in

there. We need to give him some freedom. He needs to be around other horses."

"He'll try to lord over them. The horses here are all high-strung. They're pretty good one-on-one and they manage to get along, but I don't know if Trib's ego could take it. I'm afraid of what he'd do."

"We have to trust him sometime."

Luke spoke through thinned lips. "You're big on trust, aren't you?"

Jewel rubbed against her legs and Audrey bent to pick her up. She rocked her like a baby and the cat purred quietly this time. "Yes. I'm big on trust."

Unfortunately, Luke wasn't. Not when it came to Trib and not when it came to her. He didn't have much trust in himself, either. He always did the honorable thing; that was Luke. But he didn't trust enough to free up his feelings. He wasn't a man who would let down his guard when it mattered most. He didn't trust his own instincts.

"I'll give it some thought."

She nodded and there wasn't anything more to say at the moment.

They stood facing each other in awkward silence. Audrey kept her eyes focused on him. If he wanted to turn away, he could do so, but she held firm.

Luke's eyes narrowed until they were only slivers of blue. His lips tightened and he huffed out on a breath, "I guess I'll see you later on tonight. About five o'clock?"

His enthusiasm wasn't ego-boosting. He sounded like he was going to his own hanging. Her chin went up and she couldn't hold her irritation back. "I'll be ready...*I guess*."

Luke raised his brows at her retort and then walked away.

It was clear Luke wasn't looking forward to being her escort for the evening. Pain cut through her gut at the notion. Pangs of pride withered away as she thought about how he'd tried to get out of it, to think up another solution. But in the end, Luke had done the honorable thing. He wouldn't let Sophia or Logan down. He would see her to the party, be polite all night and then make sure she arrived home safely.

She could fake an excuse and not go. But then, Sophia would be disappointed that she wasn't there. And she valued their budding friendship too much to do that.

Audrey was stuck. She had to admit she wasn't too keen on being with Luke, either, tonight. It hurt too much to be his date in name only, to know they shared earth-shattering memories in bed, and Luke wanted to forget it had ever happened. The *grave* comment wore on her nerves. He had regrets.

Well, so did she. And they burned through her. She feared she'd lost something precious with Luke, something that could never be restored. The friendship she'd always relied on was ripping away, the wound growing into a scar that would never heal. From the depths of her soul she faced a brutal and hard fact.

She couldn't be Luke's good buddy anymore.

They couldn't go back to being casual friends.

Their friendship was over.

How sad was that?

Well, at least it wasn't a monkey suit, Luke mused as he put his black jacket on over a brocade vest. He adjusted his Resistol hat on his head, straightened out his bolo tie and took a glance in the mirror.

A deep breath steadied his wrought nerves as he stared at his reflection.

He was happy for his brother. He'd found Sophia, and they would probably live out the rest of their lives blissful and content. Luke wanted to enjoy the celebration of their love and upcoming marriage. But he'd rather do that celebrating without Audrey Faith Thomas on his arm tonight.

Lord in heaven, the woman got under his skin.

For years, he'd thought of her as the kid sister he'd never

had. He'd intervened when Casey went off on her, demanding that she obey overly strict, hard-to-abide-by rules. While Casey had assumed the role of father, Luke had befriended her in a brotherly way. It was odd that all of his life, women had been his good friends. First Sophia and then Audrey.

There'd never been any sparks with Sophia, so his friendship with her wasn't difficult to maintain.

But Audrey?

Now that had come out of the blue.

It was hell for him to think of her as a woman, capable of making him act like a hormonal teenager again. Capable of making him forget who the hell she was and why he shouldn't be kissing her, touching her, making love to her.

A wince pulled his mouth down.

Enough already, Luke.

He had to stop beating himself up over it. He reminded himself that she hadn't been completely innocent. She'd brought a lot of this on herself. She'd seduced him and then turned tail and run out on him. For weeks now, she'd been living on the ranch and deceiving him.

He couldn't forget that.

With that notion firm in his mind, he headed out of his room and walked down the hallway. He braced himself and knocked on her door.

She took her sweet time opening it.

But when she finally did, his staunch resolve caved a little.

She wore sapphire blue like nobody's business.

"Hello, Luke."

He swallowed. The night was looking grim. "Wow. You look gorgeous, Audrey." He had to say it. It was the truth. Her eyes were prettier than he'd ever seen them. Blond hair framed her face in wisps of softness and then flowed down her back in long luxurious waves. The dress was made for Grecian goddesses.

She smiled and ushered him inside. "You look nice, too."

She turned away to pick up a small beaded purse from the dresser. "I'm ready. We can go now."

Luke gestured for her to lead the way. He followed behind and was grateful once they were out of the empty house and on their way. At least behind the wheel, he could concentrate on the drive and not on her. Except that she wore some sexy erotic perfume that appealed to his base instincts. Images of Audrey's wet body in the pool popped in and out of his head. He didn't want to think about the Sweet and Wicked shine on her lips, either.

He wasn't planning to get close enough to pick up that scent.

He focused his attention on the road, driving toward Tahoe and then along the scenic road up the mountain. Luke hadn't been to The Hideaway too many times. Logan had recently purchased the restaurant and if romantic and dramatic were on the agenda, then the château overlooking the hills with a view of Lake Tahoe was the place.

When they arrived, the car doors were opened by uniformed valets. One of them helped Audrey out of the car, giving her a second look. Luke couldn't blame the guy for admiring a pretty woman. Once the car was driven away, Luke escorted Audrey up the steps of the quaint château, with one hand to the small of her back. That was all the touching he'd planned on doing with her during the entire night.

She stopped and whirled around when they reached the veranda by the front doors. The sun was setting over the tips of the sugar pines and off in the distance, beams of burnished light gleamed on the lake. The Hideaway had a magnificent view of all that was glorious about Nevada.

"It's beautiful," she whispered, totally captivated by the surroundings.

"I won't be disagreeing." It was about all they hadn't disagreed upon lately. But Luke kept his tone light. He wanted Audrey to have fun tonight. She'd worked hard on Sunset

Ranch and he still considered her his friend, even if she was sorely angry at him lately.

Both of them could use a break from the tension at the ranch.

He watched her view the scenery until she'd had her fill and then escorted her into the restaurant. A gasp of pure awe escaped her throat. The place was lit with a hundred candles that gave the restaurant a warm, appealing touch. White lilies, greenery and pinecones adorned tabletops. Tall pillar candles and a gardenia centerpiece decked out the carved fireplace mantel. A three-piece band was set up off to the side. Barkeeps at a carved wood bar were serving drinks, and waiters were offering appetizers to the guests.

"Amazing," Audrey said.

Two of the younger ranch hands huddled in the corner, noticed her and gave her a wave. She returned their greeting with a genuine smile.

"The party is in full swing," he said, then spotted Logan and Sophia finishing a discussion with the caterer. "Let's say hello."

Audrey walked beside him as they made their way over to offer them congratulations.

"We should have a private toast," Luke said. He grabbed a tray of champagne flutes, giving the waitress a smile, then returned to his brother's side. "Here you go," he said, offering everyone a glass. He raised his flute high in the air. "To my brother, for finally waking up and realizing how great Sophia is for him. Something I'd known all along." He gave Sophia a wink.

"I should have realized you'd be an ass about this," Logan said, his tone light and good-natured. "But when you're right, you're right."

Everyone laughed. "Don't worry. I've got a better speech for when the time comes. This is only my warm-up," Luke joked.

"I can hardly wait."

They touched glasses with a clink and Sophia and Logan shared a special look as they sipped their drinks.

It was those special looks, those shared moments that Luke had never experienced before with a woman. He'd been burned ages ago. Yet lately he'd come to realize that those memories had faded into the woodwork of his mind. They no longer hurt. But he had begun to think he was immune to love. There was something missing in his life. Or was he being too careful, overthinking things that should come naturally?

Audrey held the flute to her mouth, ready to take a sip, when she was bumped from behind. "Oh!" Teetering on high heels, the glass dropped from her hand as she flung out her arms. Glass crashed on the floor, champagne spilling all over as she was propelled forward.

On instinct, Luke reached out, catching her fall. It was like some fancy dance move he'd seen on television with Audrey falling into his arms. Except Luke wasn't skilled with the grace of a dancer. He'd simply become her human safety net.

He brought her up tight. Her face inches from his, she looked astonished. The scent of Sweet and Wicked filled his senses, but he didn't care about that now. "Are you okay?"

She gave him a brave nod then winced in pain. "I...I think so."

Luke's teeth ground together. He balled his fists and glanced over Audrey's shoulder at the two men from the catering staff who were responsible for nearly knocking her to the ground. They were clearly oblivious and had no clue what they'd done. Luke gave her a quick kiss behind her ear and whispered, "Hang on a sec." Then he set Audrey aside gently before he approached the men.

"You boys just knocked into my date." His blood pressure pulsed when they gave him blank stares. They'd been moving tables and speaking loudly, ignorant of the guests, and as Luke got closer, he smelled alcohol on their breath. "You don't even know you hurt her. Now, before I ask you to leave, you owe her an apology."

He led the men to Audrey, who appeared pale at the moment. They hung their heads and mumbled an apology. "Okay, now move out. Do your job and be mindful of the guests."

When he turned around, Sophia was beside Audrey, holding her hand. Logan approached. "I'll go talk to them."

"They've been drinking," he said.

Logan glanced at Sophia and she nodded her approval. "They're off this job, then."

Luke was satisfied with that. He didn't have the authority to fire them, but Logan would. They had no call being drunk on the job.

"Are you hurt?" he asked Audrey. She'd really taken a hard rap to the back.

"Not really."

He wasn't sure if he believed her.

"I've been bumped by the best of them, Luke. Horses nudge me to the ground all the time."

Sophia said, "That's because they love you so much."

"And because you let them," Luke added. A smile strained his tight lips as he remembered the silly games she'd play with the horses. They would often whinny and show their affection by nuzzling her neck until she dropped to the ground in giggles. "I'll get you another drink," Luke said.

"No!" She glanced at Sophia and then at him. "I mean, not right now. I think I need some fresh air."

"Okay, fine. I'll take you outside."

"That's not necessary," she told him. "Thank you for catching me. But I think…I think I want to be alone right now."

A crew rushed over to clean up the mess while Sophia dabbed champagne from Audrey's neck and shoulders. "You're lucky. It didn't get on your dress. You look too stunning to have it ruined. Are you sure you're all right?"

"Yes, just a little shaken up."

Luke's mouth twisted. "Then let me help you—"

"Luke," she said, "please don't feel responsible for me tonight. Go, have fun. I plan to do the same in a few minutes. The band is starting up. Three couples have already beat you to the dance floor. Ask Sophia to dance while Logan is busy."

"Yes," Sophia said, angling a knowing smile at Audrey. "I feel like dancing."

Bamboozled, Luke got the message. He let Audrey go, watching her make her way to the outside deck.

"She'll be fine. You've got to stop babying her."

"Is that what you think I'm doing?" Luke asked as they walked into the middle of the room. He took his friend into his arms and they began to move as the band played a rendition of "I've Got You Under My Skin." "I'm not babying her."

"No? Then why do you look so concerned?"

"She got hurt."

"Not that much. Not enough for good-natured Luke to want to rip the heads off those guys who shoved her."

Luke narrowed his gaze and stared at Sophia. "What are you saying, exactly? And remember we're friends, so no bull."

"No bull? All right, then, but you may not want to hear this."

Luke was sorry he asked. Sophia was a straight shooter. She told it like it was. And this time, Luke wasn't sure he was ready for her honesty.

"You're attracted to Audrey. You're just realizing she's not a kid anymore and it's sort of blowing your mind a little bit. She loves the same things you love. She's pretty. Especially tonight. But because of your friendship with Casey and a code of honor you keep hidden in your back pocket somewhere, you're wired to keep your distance from her. But it's harder than you ever thought it would be."

"You're right."

Surprise lifted Sophia's brows. "I am?"

"I didn't want to hear that."

"I thought so. So, how close am I?"

"Audrey is a grown woman. Any man can see that. Casey would tear me a new one if—"

But Luke couldn't finish his thought. He'd already done things with Audrey that would give Casey a stroke—after he beat the stuffing out of him.

"If what? I know you're really not afraid of Casey."

Damn Sophia for being so astute. For knowing him so well. He sighed and twirled Sophia around, and when she came face-to-face with him again, he shrugged. "Do you blame me for not wanting to hurt her?"

Because Luke knew that he would. He'd already let things go too far between them. At one point or another, he'd be the one to walk away from her, when he found that something was missing between them. It had happened too often with too many women in his past. He didn't want to do that to Audrey. Getting further involved with her would just lead to heartache.

"No, I don't blame you, Luke. I'm your friend. I can see this is troubling you."

Sophia let him off the hook and changed the conversation to her upcoming wedding, a subject that had her bending his ear. He was grateful when Logan cut in to retrieve his fiancée.

He headed straight for the bar and ordered bourbon straight up. He spent his time chewing the fat with Hunter, Ward and a few friends from Sunset Lodge. He spoke with little Edward and his grandmother Constance shook hands with a few longtime employees, all the while keeping a vigilant eye on Audrey. She'd pretty much ignored him the whole evening, kicking it up on the dance floor with seven different partners. When she wasn't dancing, she was the center of male attention, like she was the football quarterback in a huddle. The boys seemed to hang on her every word.

When dinner was served, she sashayed her way over to the table and they made small talk throughout the meal.

"Having fun?" he asked.

"Yes, it's a nice party. I'm glad I was invited."

He glanced at her plate. She'd taken two measly bites of her prime rib and picked at her carrot soufflé and potatoes. "You didn't eat much."

"I, uh, no, I'm not too hungry tonight."

"You'd think with all the dancing you were doing, you'd have worked up an appetite."

Her gaze lowered to her plate. She picked up her fork. "I'd be a wallflower if I had to rely on you for a dance." Dainty as could be, she took a bite of food.

Luke studied her. "You're saying you want to dance with me?"

She lifted her chin defiantly. "No."

But her eyes flashed something different. The band had taken a break. Lucky thing. He didn't want to hold her in his arms tonight. Sophia had been right. He was attracted to her. More than he would admit to another living soul.

After dinner, Audrey excused herself to go to the ladies' room. Ten minutes later, when she didn't return for dessert, Luke went searching. He found her on the outside terrace, standing alone.

He sidled up next to her and braced his arms on the railing. He sipped bourbon from a highball glass. She didn't look at him, but remained quietly peering at the stars.

After a minute of silence, she spoke quietly. "I'm ready to leave. Dusty offered to take me home."

"Dusty can go to hell."

Audrey whipped her head around to stare at him with accusation in her eyes. "That was uncalled for. He was polite to offer."

Dusty had been eyeing Audrey all night. They'd danced together a few times. He worked for Sophia at the lodge and from what Luke had gathered, the guy was all right. Which bugged him ten ways to Sunday. He should let her go home and be done with it, but something inside wasn't ready to allow that to happen. "I brought you here. I'm taking you home."

"Your brother's party isn't over. I don't want to drag you away before it ends. This is an important evening for Sophia and Logan."

"So why do you want to leave so soon? Do you want to be alone with Dusty?"

Audrey's face flamed. Her eyeballs were ready to pop out of her skull. She hissed, deep and low from her throat. "How could you ask me that?"

Luke stated a fact. "He's been flirting with you all night."

"How would you know? You haven't… Oh, never mind." Audrey turned to brush past him and right on cue, the band started up again. This time it was a rendition of Elvis Presley's "Are You Lonesome Tonight."

Hell, yeah, he was.

Luke grabbed Audrey's arm before she could get away. "Dance with me."

"I don't need a pity dance, Luke."

His brows rose. He'd always admired her spunk. They stood frozen as the lyrics of loneliness and missing your sweetheart filtered through the speakers. "Then take pity on me. I want to dance with you."

Luke didn't wait for a rejection. He took her small waist in his hands and tugged her closer, then looped her arms around his neck. She gazed at him, her body a little less rigid, her eyes softening. "Luke."

His brain told him this was dangerous and stupid, but he didn't heed the warning. He'd been itching to touch her all night, despite his mental claims otherwise.

They were alone, but for a starry sky and the sound of music and muted laughter coming from inside the château. The air was crisp. The leaves of sugar pines whispered in the breeze. And Luke whispered above them into Audrey's ear, "One dance and I'll take you home."

She trembled as he brought her closer, brushing his lips over her earlobes, breathing in the scent of her hair. She was delicate now in his arms, and he took care with that. She wasn't a wallflower but a woman who had bloomed right before his eyes.

They moved then, back and forth, the soft harmony filling their senses. Audrey laid her head on his shoulder and they danced on. There was something sweet and poignant in the moment, something that Luke didn't want to end. So when the music stopped, they kept dancing, tight in an embrace, clinging to each other until sometime later their feet stopped moving and their eyes locked. Luke lifted her chin with his thumb and used it to outline the shape of her lips. Then he dipped his head and kissed her long and deep and passionately. When the kiss ended, Audrey whimpered in protest. The sound seared into his soul. He felt the same gut-wrenching sense of loss and wanted to go on kissing her. But not here, where curious onlookers might see, where any second now, his brother or Sophia might wander outside to find them together, lip-locked.

"Let's go home," he whispered with quiet urgency.

Reflecting the soft moonlight, Audrey's eyes shined with desire. "I'm ready."

Luke took her hand. He was heading for trouble, but at the moment, he didn't give a damn.

Seven

On the drive home, Audrey sat beside Luke in his car in wild anticipation of what the night would bring. They were halfway home when Audrey got a text message. "It's from Casey," she said, reading the lit-up screen.

"Oh, yeah? What's he got to say?" Luke asked quietly, giving her a smile.

Mercy. She melted into a puddle, and later she would blame his smile for her stupidity in reading the text aloud. "'I'll be coming by for a visit soon. Gotta make sure Luke's taking good care of my…uh, little sis.'" She spoke the last two words with dire dread. She was well aware of the impact that statement could make.

Luke dropped his easy smile.

"He's teasing," Audrey said softly.

But it was too late. Luke completely shut down. It was like she'd splashed ice-cold water on his face. He turned three shades of red before guilt and recrimination set in. He refused to hear her out. He refused to listen to any arguments contrary to his own thoughts on the matter. His mind was made up.

When they arrived at Sunset Ranch, he deposited her at her bedroom door. His face tight, his stance rigid, his words were strained as if he forced them out. "If you think it's easy for me to walk away from you tonight, you're sorely mistaken."

And then he did exactly that.

He closed the door and walked away.

Audrey cursed at the closed door in three different languages. The English words were the most obscene, but she managed to sputter a few choice words in Spanish and French, too.

Luke hadn't been her date tonight. Except for the last ten minutes when they'd danced and kissed out on the veranda under the stars. She'd seen a bright new world opening up to her, and hope had sprung into her heart again until Luke had decided what was best for both of them.

Now she peered at her reflection in the mirror. Her face was pale, drained of any expectation or hope. Her body sagged and her stomach ached. She wouldn't allow Luke and his stubborn ways to dictate her life anymore. If he wanted it this way, he would have it.

She glanced at the unopened pregnancy test sitting on her counter. "Not tonight," she said. She didn't want to know the outcome. She didn't want to have to face the reality of what that test would reveal. But just in case, she hadn't sipped any alcohol tonight. She'd planned on having only one drop of champagne before she'd almost been knocked to the ground.

The spill could've been a premonition, a warning not to imbibe.

She was too mentally exhausted to ponder that. She changed out of her gown and into her jeans. She pulled her hair back in a ponytail and plopped her hat on her head. "Come on, Jewel." She lifted her lazy cat up and tiptoed out of her bedroom, past Luke's room, where she heard the shower going. She hoped he needed three cold showers tonight. She continued on and walked out of the house. When she reached the barn with the cat snuggled tight to her chest, she whispered, "Just behave, Jewel."

The cat mewled softly as they approached Trib's paddock. Quietly, Audrey opened the split door. She found Trib asleep on the ground, looking innocent and gentle.

"Hi, lonely boy," she whispered.

He lifted his head.

"I brought a friend to visit you."

Bringing Jewel to the paddock had a profound effect on the horse. Not that Audrey trusted Trib enough to allow Jewel inside the stall. Heavens, both animals were too unpredictable for that, but she held Jewel in her arms and spoke sweet words of encouragement until the curious horse wandered over. The two animals stared at each other. When Jewel made a playful swat at the horse's snout, Trib didn't react, except to blink his eyes.

For the next three nights, Jewel was Audrey's accomplice. They would wait until the ranch was tucked in for the night to visit Tribute. On some animal level, Trib began to bond with Jewel. Enough so that on the fourth night, Audrey placed Jewel on the eight-inch ledge of the split door, keeping one hand on the cat. Jewel sat there in a regal pose, watching the horse. And Trib, just like all the other times, wandered over to stare at Jewel. Each night they visited, Audrey noticed Trib taking less and less time to decide to make his approach.

Progress. A bond of trust was developing. During the day, she'd visit the paddock without Jewel, and Trib would respond to her, taking treats from her hand now. Audrey felt she was moving ahead, succeeding in her attempt to tame the wildness out of the horse, yet her own personal life was at a standstill. She'd avoided Luke whenever she could and any *I might be pregnant* notions were shuffled out of her brain.

But on the fifth day that week, she took a hard fall off a stepladder, landing smack on her butt in the barn.

"Oh, no!" A jarring jolt reverberated through her body. But the pain was secondary. Fear engulfed her. What if she was pregnant and she'd injured the baby? The wake-up call rang loud in her head like the shrill alarm of a police siren. *Find out, coward. What are you waiting for? You don't want to endanger the baby, if there is a baby. You need to protect that child and keep it safe.*

That night, after work, she opened the home pregnancy test box, read the instructions and then peed on the stick.

And immediately, Audrey's life changed forever.

She was going to be a mother.

Luke, the man she'd barely spoken to for the entire week except for ranch matters, was going to be the father of her child.

A shudder worked through her system. She gripped her stomach as cautious joy swelled in her heart. She stood there, motionless and quiet. Blood pulsed through her veins rapidly, her heartbeats going a little wild. She shouldn't be surprised. She'd fooled herself into believing it wasn't so. But she'd had all the symptoms. She'd been more tired than ever lately. She couldn't explain her slight bouts of dizziness, that one ill-timed fainting spell or the nausea that seemed to come and go. Then there was the teensy-weensy little fact that she'd been late. By at least a week.

"Goodness," she whispered.

She closed her eyes and images appeared of Luke in those early rodeo days. The flashbacks played in her head like a moving picture. Luke sending her a big smile after a nine-second ride. Luke taking her side when Casey was too hard on her. Luke giving her a sweet kiss on the cheek on her birthday. Images played on and on until her legs became wobbly and weak. She made her way over to the bed to lie down. There was no sense fighting her exhaustion. She placed a protective hand over her belly and sank farther into the bed.

A text alert barked from her phone. Audrey stilled and squeezed her eyes tight. She knew it was Luke, texting her good-night. She wouldn't answer. Why change now? She'd let him think she was already asleep, like she had for the past five nights in a row.

The shock of it all overwhelmed her. She had a baby growing and thriving in her belly. She already loved the little thing.

Too bad the baby's father was the last man on earth she wanted to speak to right now.

Instead of heading back to the Slade house after work the next day, Audrey waved goodbye to Hunter and Ward at the corral and strode in the opposite direction. A walk would help clear her mind. Her nerves frazzled, her bones weary, she needed to speak to a friend more than anything else. She moved with determined steps toward the cottage that Sophia shared with Logan. Maybe, if she got lucky, she'd catch Sophia alone so that they could talk.

She wasn't five yards away from the barn when Jewel appeared and trotted in step beside her. "You feel like taking a walk with me?"

Jewel kept up with her strides, and she figured that was a resounding yes in cat talk. Jewel was astute. She knew something was up. Cats had that sixth sense about them.

When Audrey reached the cottage, she knocked on the door. The door opened slowly and little Edward appeared. Blackie jogged over amiably to rub against Edward's legs but the second the dog spotted Jewel, his big chocolate eyes rounded and then it was commotion gone wild. Blackie put his nose to the ground, sticking his rear end up, his tail whipping furiously, and took off after the cat. Jewel's back arched; poised like a big orange rainbow, she sent the dog a scathing hiss. She leaped in midair, jabbed at him with a combo of swats for all she was worth and then ran as fast as Audrey had ever seen her go.

Blackie seemed unfazed by her method of defense. He darted off after her and the merry chase was on.

Edward shouted at the dog, "Blackie, stop!"

The dog ignored him. Jewel raced over a neatly groomed bed of pansies and under hibiscus bushes. Blackie was no slacker. He followed her, barking enthusiastically until Jewel spotted an old oak tree. She climbed it in three seconds flat and by the time the dog reached the tree, it was game over. Blackie lifted up on hind legs, balancing his front paws against the base of the tree and *ruff, ruff, ruffed* his frustration.

Audrey had been betting on Jewel the entire time. The cat wouldn't let a Border collie get the best of her. Jewel sat calmly on a branch ten feet in the air, looking down her nose at the outdistanced dog.

"S-sorry," Edward said. "He's not t-trying to hurt her. He's only p-playing."

"I know," she replied to the apologetic boy. "I doubt Jewel likes his game, but she'll get over it."

After a few moments, Blackie walked off in defeat, glancing every so often at Jewel's perch on the tree as he trotted away. No doubt, the dog wanted another crack at her. When the drama was over, Audrey turned back to the boy. "How are you, Edward?"

The boy shrugged. "I'm o-kay."

"Are you having a good summer?"

He nodded. "I'm w-working."

"You are?"

"I watch Blackie and t-today I'm watering S-Sophia's plants. I brought in her m-mail, too."

"Oh, that's nice. So Sophia isn't home, then?"

"Nope. Mr. Slade t-took her on a little trip. It was a s-surprise and he asked me to w-watch the house so Sophia wouldn't worry about her plants. He g-gave me the key and everything. My grandma's coming h-here to pick me up s-soon."

Disappointment curled in her belly. Her shoulders slumped as the weight of her secret bore down on her. All the way over here, she'd thought about what she'd say to Sophia and how great it would be to unburden herself by telling her the truth. Sophia probably would've taken one look at her and guessed the truth. Oh, who was she kidding? Sophia *had* known. She'd given her the pregnancy test, recognizing the symptoms before Audrey had.

Now, Audrey longed for a pep talk and the moral support that Sophia would've given her. She needed a friend to lean on, a sympathetic ear and someone to convince her that her life wasn't a total wreck.

"I'm sure you're doing a good job," she told Edward.

His eyes lit up, and it made her feel a little bit better seeing how her encouragement gave the boy a sense of accomplishment. He'd had a rough childhood, too. Thankfully, his grandmother had intervened and the boy seemed to be thriving. Audrey had been told his speech was improving every day.

"Do you know when they'll be home?"

"T-tomorrow, I think."

"Okay. Well then, I'll just wait until then to speak with them. Oh, um, Edward. Would you mind calling Blackie? He needs to go back in the house or else Jewel will be sleeping among the oaks tonight."

The boy laughed and after Blackie cooperated, Audrey bid them farewell.

She returned to the Slade home on weak legs and with a touchy stomach, but her worst symptom wasn't physical. Her emotions were piling up, one on top of the other like a cheerleader pyramid. Any slight shift to the balance would have them all crashing down.

She entered the house with cautious steps, walking softly

and hoping to avoid Luke. A sideways glance into the parlor had her doing a quick double take.

"Hey, sis."

Her brother's familiar voice rang in her ears. His face, so strong, so caring, filled her heart with love. Forgetting her sluggishness, she raced over to where he stood in the middle of the room and flung her arms around him. "Casey!"

Sure he could be a bullheaded pain at times, but he was *her* bullheaded pain and right now her heart sang at the sight of him. His arms, tucking her in close, felt strong and comforting. "It's good to see you," she whispered.

"Same here, squirt."

Casey could call her squirt all day long for all she cared. She clung to his neck and hung on. And when she didn't protest at the nickname that usually gave her fits, he pulled her away to gaze at her curiously. "What did I do to deserve such a welcome?"

You're my big bro and I need a friend now. "What? Can't I hug my big brother?"

Casey stared at her and then blinked while taking a full step back to give her a good once-over. Her arms dropped to her sides and Audrey felt a keen sense of loss without him hugging her.

His eyes touched on her pale complexion and then his gaze shifted to scrutinize her body. She tried to lift her sagging shoulders and hide the shakiness of her wobbly legs. A scowl formed on his face and his loving expression immediately transformed to concern. "You don't look good, sis. What's the matter, honey?"

The cheerleader toppled from the top of the heap. All balance was gone. Her pent-up emotions unraveled and tears sprung from her eyes. "Oh, Casey."

She fell into his chest and unleashed her sobs.

Slowly, he brought her into the circle of his arms again. "It's…okay," he said as if he didn't know how to soothe the grown-up version of his little sister. He patted her back and hushed her quietly. "Why are you crying, sweetheart?"

She continued to sob, her unbanked tears coming as a surprise to her, as well. She wasn't sure what or how to tell him.

His booming voice shook. "Are you…ill? Did you come here to hide it from me? Tell me, Audrey Faith. You're scaring the life out of me."

She began shaking her head. Casey feared for her life. Oh, heavens. He'd gotten it all wrong. Her brother always looked out for her. She didn't always appreciate it but now she realized how much he'd sacrificed for her. How much he worried over her. She caught her breath between sobs. "No…I'm not ill. I'm fine. It's just that…I'm, I'm…*pregnant*."

It was the first time she'd said the words aloud. They felt strange to her ears and the gravity of her situation and Casey's reaction—a shift in his body temperature from warm to ice-cold—made her feel it all the more. The news paralyzed him a moment.

He didn't move a muscle.

After long, drawn-out moments, he spoke through clenched teeth. "I'll crush that Toby Watson."

"It's not Toby's," she said in a rush.

Out of the corner of her eye, she saw movement at the parlor doorway. A figure, tall and lean and good-looking as sin, strode into the room to stand beside Casey.

Luke's gaze bore down on her. He rasped, "Audrey, you're having my baby?"

Audrey faced him. "Oh, Luke."

Casey's mouth dropped open. He didn't miss the implication. He swiveled his head to glare at the man standing next to him. "You're asking my sister if she's having your kid?"

Luke ignored Casey. His full attention was on her. "Answer me."

Audrey opened her mouth, but before she could utter her reply, Casey's fist met with Luke's face. "You son of a bitch."

Eight

The punch surprised Luke, and he staggered back. He rebounded quickly and came at Casey with his fists clenched and ready, but at the last minute, he backed off.

"Come on," Casey said, waving both hands, egging him on and inviting a fight. "Take a punch so I can knock you to Carson City."

Luke glared at Casey and rubbed his face where he'd been hit. His cheek was swollen. There would be a nasty bruise. "Back off, Casey. I'm not going to fight you."

Casey bellowed, "The hell you're not."

Audrey's tears stopped flowing. She'd made a big mess of everything and she didn't know how to fix it, but she certainly didn't want the two men she loved most in the world to have a barroom brawl in the middle of the parlor. "Stop it. Casey, you're still recovering from a broken back."

He granted her a sideways glance. "Hell, Audrey, I'm fine. Now be quiet."

"I won't be quiet. You're not fine, and you're not going to beat Luke up."

"Like he could," Luke said, puffing his chest out.

The two men sized each other up. Both of them were acting like juveniles.

Casey got in Luke's face. "You're a bastard, Luke."

"No, he's not." Audrey was angry about Luke's stubborn and far-reaching code of honor, but she wouldn't stand here and allow Casey to make assumptions about Luke that weren't true. "None of this is Luke's fault. It was all my doing."

Casey snorted as if she'd handed him a load of manure. "It's always the guy's fault, Audrey Faith. No matter what you did, he did worse. I doubt you forced him into it."

Oh, but she had. Almost. She'd seduced him. "He didn't even know it was—"

"I don't want to hear details, for pity's sake." Casey cut her off, his face pinched tight.

Luke stepped in between her and Casey and spoke directly to her brother. "You're right. I'm a bastard. You trusted me and I blew that trust to hell."

"Luke!" Audrey couldn't believe her ears. Luke was being Luke and manning up for her sake. Luke wouldn't let her lose face with her brother. But the truth was, he wasn't at fault, and his friendship with Casey hung in the balance. "Let me explain it to him. Let me tell him how it all happened the first time. You see, Casey, I was coming—"

Luke turned to her and put up a hand, a warning in his voice. "Don't, Audrey. He doesn't want the details."

"I surely don't."

Luke's cheek was turning a shade of purple. He kept his voice calm, trying to diffuse the situation. His eyes softened on her. "Are you carrying my baby?"

She nodded. "I haven't seen a doctor yet, but the pregnancy test is positive. I have all the symptoms."

Luke swallowed.

Casey muttered a curse under his breath.

A beat ticked by and then the two men spoke in unison.

"You're marrying me," Luke said.

"You're marrying him," Casey said.

The two of them looked at each other, none too friendly, but nodded in agreement.

"Damn right you're marrying her," Casey muttered.

"You just heard me ask her, didn't you?"

"Then it's settled," Casey said.

Both of them turned to her. She faced two stubborn-set jaws on men who had no clue how much they'd just hurt her. She didn't think it possible, but her heart broke even more. Casey loved her and cared about her, but he'd been dictating the terms of her life for too long. She didn't want or need his approval on her decisions. Though if she had his blessing, she'd be grateful and happy about it. But she certainly wasn't going to allow him to make the biggest decision of her life for her.

Luke, on the other hand, didn't love her. That said it all, didn't it? In Audrey's fantasy world, Luke loved her and wanted to marry her and live out his life with her. But that wasn't the case. She couldn't let him demand that she enter into a marriage based on his noble sense of morality. She loved him too much for that. A lopsided marriage for the baby's sake wouldn't make anyone happy. The last thing Luke wanted was a loveless marriage. And the last thing she wanted was to live her life without his love.

Finally, it dawned on her. She deserved better. No more halves in her life. She'd had half a family, living without the love of a mother and father all these years. She'd had half a school life, too—tagging behind Casey on the rodeo circuit while her high school friends were having fun, getting into trouble and learning how to deal with impending adulthood. She'd had half an education, her studies being cut short by Casey's back injury.

She'd sacrificed for him and wanted to help him recover, in much the same the way he'd sacrificed his life to raise her. Neither of them had had a choice.

But this time, finally, Audrey did have a choice. This time she was old enough to make a stand for what she wanted out of life. This time, she had something to say about it.

She didn't want Luke if he didn't love her. She'd never deny him his child. They would work something out later on. But for now, Audrey's decision was seared in her mind as the way it had to be.

"Casey," she said firmly, her sobs from five minutes ago well forgotten, "nothing is settled. I'm almost twenty-five years old. I love you, but you're not my keeper. I make my own decisions."

She turned away from Casey to look straight into Luke's eyes. "Luke, that was hardly a proposal. You didn't ask. But my answer would've been the same. No, I will not marry you."

Never in her life would she have dreamed of turning down Lucas Slade's offer of marriage.

Both men's mouths moved. They started flapping their gums, jawing at her, but this time, Audrey didn't listen. Her decision was final and nothing either of them could say at this point would change her mind. "I'm exhausted. I'm going to bed. I don't want to be disturbed." She held her head high, regally—a lesson learned from Jewel—and pointed a finger at both of them. "Don't argue after I'm gone. For heaven's sake, you two are friends. Promise me you'll get along."

Casey grumbled.

Luke muttered something.

The two of them wouldn't look at each other.

"Okay, I have your promise," she said, darting each one a purposeful glance before she walked out of the room.

Luke and Casey sat on the front steps of the porch, a half-empty bottle of Scotch whiskey between them. A pinkish blaze of light lowered on the horizon. Dusk's long fingers touched the earth and settled around the ranch.

Branches fluttered from a bird's flight. Horses whinnied, and off in the distance an owl hooted. Ranch sounds carried to Luke's ears as the land whispered good-night, but Luke wasn't ready to turn in. Hell, he had the other half of the bottle to polish off.

Casey refused to budge. He sat still as a stone, mumbling as he imbibed the good stuff.

"I'm never gonna forgive you for this." Casey poured an inch of whiskey down his throat and then reached for the bottle to fill up his glass again.

"I know."

"She's a good kid." Casey's gravelly voice rose an octave. "Damn you, Luke," he said for the tenth time.

Luke should be burning in hell from all the damning Casey was doing.

"You were the good one," he said. "I'd be breaking all the rules and you'd be right there, Mr. Clean, always picking up the pieces. Always doing the right thing. Why the hell didn't you do the right thing with my sister? Why the hell did you knock her up?"

Luke sipped his whiskey, looking down at the amber liquor in his glass. "Wasn't intentional."

Hell, no, it wasn't. He hadn't set out to touch Audrey much less get her pregnant. The concept of fatherhood was still foreign to him. He struggled with it. He was going to have a baby. With Audrey. Everything inside him said he had to do the right thing, so he'd demanded marriage of her. But a loveless marriage was the last thing he'd wanted. All of his life he'd planned on something more than his father had with his mother. He'd waited for that zing, for that missing piece of the puzzle, for that extra bounce in his step when he thought about a woman. When it didn't happen, he just figured he needed to wait some more. But now, the baby changed everything.

"I should've knocked you out."

Luke drew breath into his lungs and spoke quietly. "You couldn't if you tried."

"Landed a pretty dang mean right hook, though."

"You sucker punched me."

"I'm not sorry."

"I got that the first three times you told me."

"First thing tomorrow, I'm gonna pack up and go. And I'm taking my kid sister with me."

That was not going to happen. Luke wasn't going to let Casey badger Audrey into leaving. She was pregnant with his child. They had things to work out. Luke's fist balled up. He spoke with menace in his voice. "You can go anytime you want. But Audrey's not leaving until I talk to her."

"She told you she's not marrying you."

"And you think you're gonna bully Audrey into leaving with you?"

"I don't bully her."

"You've been bullying her since the day I met you. She was too young and dependent on you to fight back. But, man, you were clueless when it came to her. Audrey's not a kid. She's all grown-up. Somehow your radar missed that, Case. She's old enough to make up her own mind about things. She's old enough to decide about her life and her future. I slept with her, yes. It was a mistake on my part, but believe me when I say this—she made her decision to be with me. She wasn't forced or bullied. So you may think I'm a bastard, and I may very well be, but don't think for a minute I'm going to let you ramrod her into going home with you."

Luke rose then. The world tipped a little. His head spun, but Luke knew his limits and this wasn't it. He wasn't hammered enough not to see the truth. He had to stand his ground now. He pointed his finger right down the nose of his friend.

"You let Audrey decide what she wants to do." He turned and grabbed the door handle. Right before he walked inside, he added, "And don't you even think about getting behind the wheel of your car tonight."

Casey poured the last drop of Scotch into his glass and muttered, "Hell, Luke. What do you take me for? I'm not that dang stupid."

Luke grinned, satisfied, although he didn't know why he was feeling so darn good. He had a reluctant bride on his hands and a baby on the way.

In the morning, Audrey walked into the kitchen at the usual time. Luke was at the table, sipping coffee, the food on his plate untouched. He gazed up with bloodshot eyes. The bruise on his face had faded some, but it hadn't gone away. There was a round blotch of color just under his right eye. She wondered what Ellie had said about it or if she'd asked at all.

Luke looked sorely hungover. He'd taken the news of her pregnancy like a man, demanding marriage and then drinking himself into oblivion when she'd refused his nonproposal.

"Ellie made breakfast," he said.

A dish of French toast, scrambled eggs and honey-smoked bacon greeted her. Well…thank goodness the sugary and savory scents mingling in the air didn't make her queasy. She might actually be able to handle a bit of breakfast this morning.

"Would you like some coffee?" the plump, white-haired woman asked, coming toward the table with a steaming pot in her hand.

"No, thanks, Ellie. I'll have juice today. Everything looks delicious."

The housekeeper nodded and turned on her heel. A few seconds later, a glass of orange juice appeared in front of her. "There you go. And for you, Luke?"

"I'll stick with coffee this morning. If you're through here, I'd like to speak with Audrey privately."

"Surely," Ellie said, pouring more coffee into his cup. "I'll be back later to straighten up the kitchen."

"I've got it, Ellie," Audrey said. The housekeeper was a one-woman dynamo. Every pot and pan she'd used to cook the meal was already cleaned and put away. Just the tabletop dishes remained. "There's just a few things here. I'll load the dishwasher."

"Well, thank you," Ellie said, wiping her hands on a dish towel, giving her a smile. "You're a dear."

The housekeeper left the room and they sat silently. That was fine with Audrey. She took a few bites of crisp bacon and forked her way through half a piece of one-inch-thick cinnamon-and-pecan French toast. Her stomach didn't rebel and she considered it a good way to start off the morning.

"Casey leave?"

She nodded. "I said goodbye to him this morning."

"He try to get you to go with him?"

"We talked," she said. Her brother hadn't pressed the issue. They'd actually had a civilized adult conversation this morning. She hadn't gone into a lot of detail, but she explained to him about what happened at the cabin and owned up to the blame. Casey didn't fully buy it. Her brother didn't want to let Luke off the hook, yet he hadn't argued with her. She'd asked him to leave the ranch and let her finish the job she came here to do. It was clear Casey didn't want to do that, leaving her in the hands of Evil Luke and all, but he finally nodded in agreement. It surprised the hell out of her when he kissed her cheek, got in his car and drove off without giving her a lecture.

"And you're still here."

"Casey doesn't decide my life, Luke. I think I made myself clear yesterday." She pushed her plate away. Her stomach couldn't handle any more. "I've got a job to do. I plan on finishing what I started."

He nodded and sipped coffee. "I'm glad you're not leaving. I want you to stay."

Endorphins sprang free and she was struck with impossible hope and joy. She fought the warm feeling for all she was worth. Luke was only saying that because of the baby, she reminded herself. A short time ago, he regretted her being on Sunset Ranch.

"I plan to stay."

"Well, then, it's settled."

Luke could be an ass at times, she decided. "Only because *I'm* settling it."

His eyes narrowed on her. They looked patriotic—*red,* white and blue. "Touchy."

"Yeah, well…that's what happens to pregnant women. We get touchy."

"I'll remember that. Are you an expert now?"

"I've been reading up." On the internet. There was an abundance of knowledge there, but some of it was scary stuff. She made a decision to look up the facts only and not get sucked into the thousands of pregnancy blogs and nightmare stories or else she wouldn't sleep nights. It was a classic case of TMI. "I made an appointment with a doctor."

"A local doctor?"

"Yes." She nodded. "For now."

Relief registered on his face. "I'd like to go with you."

At least it wasn't a demand. "I figured you would. Okay, we'll go together. The appointment is late tomorrow morning."

"Thanks."

"I'm not going to keep you away from the baby, Luke."

For all her misgivings, Luke was a good man, and he'd be a wonderful father. She hadn't any doubts about it. "But you won't marry me?"

The breath whooshed out of her. Tears stung behind her eyes. How many times would she have to refuse the very thing she'd been dreaming about her entire life? How many times would she have to hold her head up high and fight for the one thing she wanted, above all else, for her and her baby…a life filled with true love. "I…can't."

"Why not, Audrey? We're having a baby. That changes everything."

"Your parents had a loveless marriage, Luke. And you never wanted that for yourself. They married for the child's sake."

"They lived a decent life. They raised a family. What they had wasn't terrible."

A sigh climbed up from the depth of her heart. "Did you just hear yourself?" The sting behind her eyes burned now and she struggled not to break down in tears. Audrey couldn't resign herself to being a wife to Luke that way. "Do you want something that only isn't *terrible?*"

Luke stared at her. He heaved a heavy sigh. His shoulders rose and fell. "We'll both love the baby."

Audrey stood up and leaned over the table. Sophia told her she'd know when the time was right. She'd know when she had to tell Luke the ultimate truth. And the time had come. Audrey couldn't put it off anymore. She'd lived with this for ten years. It was finally time to come clean. Luke was beginning to soften her resolve. She was beginning to think about how easy it would be to marry him. To live in this big house and see him every day, raise their child together and get along with him the same way they always had, as friends.

She warred with it in her head for long, drawn out moments. It was the hardest decision she ever had to make. And it was breaking her heart a thousand times over. But she couldn't go through with it. Luke had been her dream, one she would completely sully by going halfway. It had to be all or nothing with Luke. No halves when it came to Lucas Slade.

"You don't love me, Luke."

Luke's breath caught in his throat. Her bluntness surprised him. He rose to face her from across the table.

She was glad he stood. Glad she could look him straight in the eyes and give him the truth. "But you see…I love you. I have for ten years. It wasn't just a childhood crush. It wasn't just a fascination with my big brother's buddy. I have loved you for so long, and so hard, for so many years, it's killing me to pretend I don't. You're the only man I've ever wanted. I didn't set out for any of this to happen. I surely didn't intend to get pregnant, Luke. But that night at the cabin, when I walked into the room and saw you there, I realized that if I walked away, I might blow the only chance I had with you. I might've walked away from something I had dreamed about for years. It was important for me to be with you that night. It was my chance to show you how much I cared for you.

"Did you ever ask yourself why I climbed into bed with you that night? Did you think I'd lay with any man sleeping in that bed? Did you think I was a slut? You never once considered that I might have true feelings for you, Luke. You never once looked at me as anything other than a friend, your buddy's little sister. I have strong feelings for you. I love you with all my heart. And I'm having your baby."

Audrey set her hand on the new life growing inside her even as tears wet her cheeks. "We will not go into this halfway. We want one hundred percent of you. We want all-in. We want to be your pot of gold."

Luke swallowed and blinked his eyes. "Audrey."

Audrey's voice began to crack. "I will n-never keep you from your child, Luke. And I wish to heaven that you l-loved me, but you don't, so I won't m-marry you. I hope you can understand that. Now, I h-have work to do. I'll s-see you later."

She turned to leave, wiping tears with the sleeve of her blouse as she headed out the door.

"Audrey, wait!"

Luke's plea only stopped her for a second. She squeezed her eyes closed and stood waiting for Luke to say what she needed to hear.

When he offered nothing else, Audrey turned to face his blank stare. "I have waited, Luke. For ten years."

Then she exited the room.

Nine

Luke canceled his meetings for the morning and changed into a pair of washed-out jeans and a T-shirt. He slipped his hat on his head and walked to the barn. He found Ward there, saddling up the dapple-gray Andalusian gelding that would be leaving the ranch in three days. He'd been sold to a Frenchman who wanted the good-natured horse for his twelve-year-old daughter.

"Hey, Luke, I'm just about ready to exercise him. You need me for something?"

Luke stared at the horse that he'd admired for a long time. "How about I take this one out this morning?"

Ward gave him a quizzical stare. "You want to take Caliber out? Well, sure thing. I'll take one of the Arabians. You want company on the ride?"

Luke didn't blame Ward for questioning him. He rarely rode the horses he intended to sell. Usually Luke rode his own mare, a fast yet gentle bay mare of fine breeding named Nutmeg. "Not this time, Ward. Appreciate the offer, though. I just want to take him out by myself. Say goodbye, you know?"

Ward gave the animal a firm, affectionate pat. "Yeah, I know. Gonna miss him. He's got spirit, this one, but he's a pushover with kids. Edward comes by to see him and the horse has such a tender way with him. That little girl's gonna be real happy on her twelfth birthday."

Luke nodded. He mounted the horse and rode off without saying any more. He wasn't much in a mood for small talk.

He'd tried to small talk his way with Audrey last night with a text message.

Just making sure you're feeling well.

After the bombshell she'd dropped about having his baby, Luke had been at his wits' end. Yet, he'd had to give Audrey the time and space she needed. It wasn't as if he didn't need time, too. This whole thing had been a weird twist of fate and now an innocent child's future was at stake.

I'm feeling okay. Going to bed now.

was her curt reply, and Luke had gotten the hint.

This morning, Audrey had dropped her second bombshell. Apparently, one wasn't enough for her. He didn't know which one had shocked him more. Now, not only did he have an un-born child to deal with, he had Audrey's vow of love plagu-ing his thoughts.

Summer heat drew down on him. Luke lowered the brim of his hat and clucked his tongue. The Andalusian took off at a run. Caliber's long legs ate up ground and Luke's hat nearly blew off his head as the animal flew across the acre-age. Out beyond the pasture, with the house long forgotten in the distance, Luke thought his head would clear. He thought everything would become as transparent as glass or at least as clear as a murky, old barn window.

Solutions didn't magically appear.

One thing kept coming back to his mind. One thing knocked him upside the head over and over again and continued to plague him.

Audrey loved him.

He hadn't seen it coming.

He was a damn fool for being so dense.

Her heartbreaking confession this morning left him dumbfounded. And numb. He'd hurt Audrey in the worst possible way and the sad thing about it was he would continue to hurt her. Because he didn't feel the same way about her.

He brought Caliber to a trot along a path that led to a cropping of apple trees. The fruit wasn't edible yet, the balls were hard and green and the size of a walnut. He dismounted, his boots hitting the earth as hard as his heart was heavy. He ground-tethered the horse and stared out on Slade land from under the shade of a tree.

Why was it that grown-up Luke Slade had never loved a woman?

The horse snorted, his breaths labored and deep from the long run. Luke stared at him for a minute, sorry to see the gelding go. He was a beautiful animal and a good addition to the Slade ranch. Every single one of the ranch hands, the wranglers especially, remarked on the horse's good nature. Even Audrey had called him a sweetheart.

Which was a lot more than she'd called him lately.

Luke took a big swallow. In that moment, he realized something. He'd seen it first in Ward's puzzled expression when he'd offered to take Caliber out. Now, it was as if someone had taken a rag and wiped that old barn window clean. There was clarity that Luke had never seen before. And the news wasn't good.

He had a flaw.

Well, damn, he had many. He didn't think he was all that, but this blemish in his character got his spurs to jingling, as his father would say.

Luke thought back to when he was a boy of six and a sleek, beautiful colt named Smoke was born on the ranch. It had been love at first sight as far as Luke was concerned. He'd eaten, slept and breathed for love of that colt. His dad had warned him not to get too attached because Smoke was bred of champions and he would be sold off. He'd go to a good home, Randall Slade had said. Luke pretended he'd understood, but that hadn't stopped his fascination with the horse. In his young heart, he'd never believed Smoke—the colt he'd loved since the moment the foal was brought into the world—would really be leaving the ranch.

Then one day six months later, Luke's heart had nearly broken in two when he saw Smoke being loaded into a trailer. He remembered running as fast as his little legs would take him, chasing after that trailer, crying and calling Smoke's name. His father had looked at him with regret in his eyes. As if to say, *I'm sorry, son, but I warned you.*

Luke had cried himself to sleep for one entire month, learning a life lesson that was probably way too hard for a six-year-old boy to fully comprehend. But he'd understood the heartache. And the pain inflicted.

After that, Luke had admired the horses on the ranch from afar. As a boy, he would feed them, ride them when necessary, groom and muck their stalls, all chores his rigid old man required. But he would never allow himself to get close to them. To make a lasting bond. He'd come to realize the hard facts of life on a horse farm. It was the family business. Those gorgeous bays and palominos and black stallions... they would be all be leaving eventually. They'd be sold outright and Luke would never see them again.

The only exception was Tribute. Somehow, that stallion had gotten under his skin. Luke had tried to tame him and had been persistent in that pursuit. The why of it wasn't clear in his mind, but he'd felt a kinship with the spirited animal and looked upon him as a challenge.

Luke focused back on the present, his mind racing, thinking befuddled and crazy thoughts. He squeezed his eyes closed and then muttered a curse.

You're a coward, Luke.

A big, freaking coward.

Thoughts whirled in his head and truths came to light.

He feared getting hurt. He'd never made lasting bonds. He'd protected himself from future pain at all costs. It was a pattern in his life and not a truth he liked facing. But it was there, underneath all the other garbage in his mind.

Luke was always the first one to walk away from a woman. Images popped into his head of the women in his past and the relationships he'd refused to work on. His noncommittal attitude and his willingness to call it a day when things got rough or when things looked like they were getting too serious played over in his mind.

He'd done the same with Audrey. And she'd come with an additional warning tag—she was Casey's sister. Yet of all the women Luke had been with, the only one he'd want to carry his child and spend his future with was…Audrey. That was a good thing, wasn't it? Marriage and parenthood with her were doable. He liked Audrey. She was a good friend. She was pretty. Beautiful, he would say. And she came from the same background as he did. She was a country girl and loved ranch life. The notion of life with her *wasn't terrible.*

Crap.

Dang it if Audrey wasn't right about him. It was a sad state of affairs. He shook his head and muttered, "You are sorely jaded, Luke Slade."

He mounted Caliber and rode the horse back to the ranch at a slow, easy trot. When he arrived at the stables, he decided to groom Caliber himself, wash him down and currycomb him. He checked his legs and picked out a pebble from his shoe and then let the horse feed from a bucket of oats. He slipped the gelding a few sugar cubes, too. His efforts raised eyebrows among the ranch hands and he also caught Audrey, mother of his child and woman who refused to marry him, staring at him a time or two.

Audrey tiptoed out of the house just after midnight with Jewel at her heels. Her work with Trib was paying off. It seemed the horse looked upon Jewel as an equal and somewhat of a friend. What choice did the stallion have? Jewel was the only game in town. Hopefully, it was more than that. Hopefully, Trib's temperament was mellowing and he was beginning to trust the both of them. That's all she wanted. Some trust from the horse.

Quiet as a church mouse, she entered the barn and opened the top half of the paddock door. Immediately, Jewel jumped up on the ledge with the grace of, well…a cat, to take her regal pose and greet her new friend.

Meow.

The second Trib spotted her, he wandered over. He settled right by the paddock door and stood nose to nose with the cat. Audrey whispered, "Hi, boy. That's right. Come closer. We won't hurt you."

The horse shifted his gaze to her for a moment, then back to the cat.

Carefully, Audrey dug into her pocket and came up with half a dozen sugar cubes in her palm. She arranged them carefully and slowly brought her hand toward the horse's mouth. "A treat for you."

Trib craned his neck and turned his head toward her hand. Out came his long pink tongue to lick her palm and gobble up the sugar cubes. Audrey released a breath. Success. "You are lonely," she whispered. "Well, don't you worry. We're here now."

Maybe it was her imagination, but the wariness that she'd come to expect from Trib was gone. At least for right now. She wanted so badly to let this horse know he had nothing to fear from her and that he didn't need to guard himself quite so carefully when she was around.

Making progress with Trib helped ease her heartache about Lucas Slade. At least she had these nights to look forward to. At least she felt needed and wanted by the very horse that had severely injured her baby's father.

How strange was that?

That night, Audrey fell into an exhausted sleep. In the morning, she rose and dressed, readying for her first appointment with the obstetrician who would be treating her while she lived on Sunset Ranch.

She walked into the kitchen and found Luke there, seated at the table. He lifted his beautiful face, his blue eyes brightening the second they landed on her. Emotion rocked and rolled inside her belly, which wasn't at all fair, since she'd just gotten over her morning sickness. She'd never get through these next few weeks if Luke continued to look at her like that.

"Morning," he said.

"Good morning."

She distracted herself by looking at the big breakfast Ellie had whipped up. Flapjacks and eggs sat waiting for her along with a bowl of fresh late-summer fruit. She turned to Ellie, who was wiping a dish at the sink. "Looks great, Ellie."

"I hope so. I've got more coming, if you're inclined."

Ellie liked to feed people. "Oh, no, I'm sure this is plenty." She took a seat at the table.

"You sleep well?" Luke asked, always the gentleman. Though Audrey figured she looked like heck since her secret work with Trib kept her awake half the night. Afternoon naps were not overrated and she'd managed to slip a few in this week to make up for the loss of sleep.

"Yes, I did. Thank you."

He nodded.

Lime-scented aftershave wafted in the air and teased her nostrils. Luke always smelled so good. He wore a crisp black-and-white-checked shirt tucked into the waistband of brand-new Wrangler jeans.

They ate in silence, both aware of Ellie's presence. Audrey hadn't told anyone but Casey, Sophia and Luke about her pregnancy. She was certain Ellie didn't know and she wanted to keep the news close at hand for a little while longer. Luke would want to tell his brothers, she was sure, but when he thought it best.

When Ellie excused herself from the kitchen, Luke lifted his eyes to her. "I put aside my work for the morning, so I can drive you into town for the appointment. I'm…uh, well, I want to support you and let you know you're not in this alone."

Tears stung behind Audrey's eyes. It was a beautiful thing to say, yet somehow those words spoken from Luke, the man she loved, made her ache inside. "I know. You're too decent to abandon me."

He straightened in his seat as if she'd insulted him. "I'd never do that. I asked you to marry me."

Audrey glanced away. Luke just didn't get it.

And later that morning, after driving into Silver Springs, they met with Dr. Amanda Ayers. After an examination that Luke insisted on attending, the fine doctor confirmed the pregnancy, giving them both insights as to what to expect in the coming months, along with a list of instructions to follow. The reality of her motherhood sank in like a sledgehammer pounding wood.

"I guess there's no getting around it," Audrey said, as Luke took her hand and guided her out of the doctor's office.

Luke smiled. "The pregnancy? Only way I know happens nine months from now."

Gladness filled her heart. At least Luke was taking it like a man. He'd fully participated in the discussion with Dr. Ayers and now he seemed to be adjusting well to becoming a father. She wouldn't go so far as to say he was happy about it. The situation wasn't ideal. The details of her life were murky at best. If she decided to move back to Reno, the baby would have two homes and parents who weren't together, but it pleased Audrey to see Luke's gradual acceptance. "That's seven months and one week from now, buster."

Luke gave her hand a little squeeze and chuckled as he opened the car door for her. He had no idea what his touch did to her or the loss she felt when he let go.

"Yeah. You gotta forgive my math skills."

She slid into her seat and strapped her seat belt on, glancing up at him. "Hopefully, the baby will have my brains."

Luke didn't miss a beat. "As long as he has my good looks, we're golden." He winked and closed the door before she could think of a witty retort.

They left Silver Springs in the dust. And once out of town and onto the open road, Luke reached over to take her hand in his. Bone-melting warmth spread through her system. Did he know what he was doing to her? Was it a deliberate attempt to soften her and get her to change her mind about marrying him?

He gazed into her eyes then and for several magical moments she saw something new, something different in the way he looked at her. She wasn't imagining it. There was a connection now, fragile as it was, and the hope in her heart was becoming a tangible thing.

Mercy.

He paid attention to the road for the next ten minutes and then turned to face her again. "I'm pretty darn hungry." The caress in his eyes was still there. "Would you have lunch with me? I know this little place just off the road that I think you'd like."

She didn't have to think twice. Her appetite for food and for Luke had returned. "Would love to."

Content, he made a right turn onto a single-lane highway and parked in front of the Chipmunk Café.

She reread the sign above the cabin-esque building and gave a slight shake of the head.

"What is this place?"

"You'll see."

He helped her out of the car and held her hand as they strode into the wood cabin diner. Audrey took a look around and her mouth dropped open. Her gaze roamed over tables and bench seats made of molded plastic that resembled split-wood logs. The walls were decorated with oversize walnuts, woodsy foliage and greenery. Off in one corner was a children-only section where little ones crawled into a simulated underground chipmunk burrow and sat on stools that stood less than one foot high to eat their meals. Other game areas were strategically placed throughout the large dining hall that kept kids racing from one to the other with big smiles beaming on their faces.

"I heard Dr. Ayers say that protein is good for the baby," Luke said. "I hope you like nuts and seeds, because every dish here is made with them. Either in the recipe or crushed and sprinkled on top as a coating. My favorite is the peanut-crusted hamburger."

Audrey felt her smile widen. She already loved this place. "How long have you been coming here?"

"Ever since I was a kid. Wasn't often enough for me back then. It was a special treat if Mom and Dad agreed to bring us here. Dad hated the noise and Mom was allergic to nuts."

"Oh, wow, Luke. I don't remember you ever talking about this place."

Luke looked around. "There's an empty booth. Wanna try it?"

"Of course." She wouldn't think of disappointing him.

Luke put his hand to her waist and guided her across the room, fending off three small children racing toward the bur-

row. Luke smiled like a little boy when a waitress dressed in
a furry russet-colored chipmunk costume came to take their
order. Audrey opted for the candied-walnut chicken salad and
Luke ordered his favorite burger.

During the entire meal Luke rattled on and on about the
baby and the things he wanted to do with him or her. Audrey found herself caught up in the enthusiasm and they both
agreed, once the baby got old enough, they would put the
Chipmunk Café on their radar.

That warm light in Luke's eyes didn't diminish throughout the meal or on the drive home. Something was definitely
different with Luke today. He kept finding ways to touch her.
To slip her hand into his or to spread his palm across her back
as they walked along. But she didn't place much faith in it.
He was getting excited about the baby. Not her. Never her.

She'd pretty much convinced herself of that.

They entered the house together, Luke closing the door
behind them. She took a step toward the hallway that led to
her room and felt a gentle pull on her arm. A strong hand
slipped down to her wrist and she turned to look into Luke's
incredibly handsome face.

"Thank you," he said, "for letting me come today."

His grasp on her wrist tightened as he drew her closer. She
drifted to him as if on a windswept cloud. "It's important that
you be there. You're, uh, the baby's father."

Sincerity touched his eyes and he gave a slight nod.

"Thanks for the Chipmunk Café," she whispered, her ridiculous heart beating like mad.

"I had fun."

"So did I. It's a wild place for kids."

"For some grown-ups, too," he said with a cocky grin that
brought out all of his boyish charm.

"Well, I'd…uh, I'd better get changed. I have wor—"

Luke glanced at her mouth. Then a smile broadened his
lips and he bent his head. She didn't move. She didn't step

back. Fool that she was, she wanted this. The second his lips touched hers, all the warning bells ringing in her head went on mute. A tiny whimper rose from her throat. Luke deepened the kiss until her breaths came fast and heavy. Thoughts of pushing him away entered, then fled her mind. She couldn't breathe, much less think.

She curled her arms around his neck. He pulled her closer. His hand cupped the back of her head and strands of her hair flowed over his arm. The kiss went on a good, long time.

Finally, Luke allowed her to come up for air.

The impact of his passionate kiss pleasantly stung her lips. She stared at him, trembling. "Wh-what was that all about?"

"Sweetheart," Luke said, his brows gathering and a question in his expression, "I wish I knew."

"Good news," Logan said, walking into Sophia's office at Sunset Lodge and interrupting Luke's conversation with his good friend. Sophia not only managed the place but was now a full partner. "Justin will be home in time for our wedding. He'll be here in a few weeks."

Luke was glad to hear it. Justin had been gone for too long. Luke and everyone else at Sunset Ranch missed him. "Don't you knock?"

"Why should I knock on my fiancée's door?" Logan asked with a wry smirk. "I didn't expect to find you here wasting her time."

Luke caught Sophia grinning at Logan. The two of them were ridiculously happy. "She was my best friend before she was your fiancée."

"Old news, bro. I'm so tickled about our little brother coming home, I won't even let you rile me," Logan said.

"You mean the little brother who could probably whoop both our butts without breaking a sweat?"

"That's the one. Just don't let him hear you admit that."

"You think I'm crazy?" Luke asked.

Logan strode over to where Sophia was sitting behind her desk to give her a kiss.

"Looks like there's good news for all three of the Slade brothers," Sophia said. She shot a quick look at Luke, giving him the opening he needed. "Luke was just about to tell me something important."

He sat in a comfy leather seat at an angle to her, his legs stretched out, his arm braced on the edge of the desk as he toyed with a ballpoint pen. *Click, click, click.*

"Oh, yeah?" Logan took a seat beside him and shifted his gaze to him. "Our wedding, Justin's homecoming and what else?"

Luke had to face his brother with the truth and it pained him to admit that doing the right thing by Audrey wasn't in his hands. She held all the cards. "Audrey and I are having a baby."

Logan's mouth dropped open. He blinked a few times, absorbing the shocking news, and Luke couldn't fault Logan his reaction. Audrey had always been off-limits. It was an unspoken rule, a code of honor between friends. At least in the Slade world it was. "You and Audrey? I'll be damned. Does Casey know?" Logan examined his face. "Oh, wait a minute, is that what happened to your cheek?"

Luke's mouth twisted. The bruise was barely visible anymore but his brother was as sharp as a tack. "He wasn't too happy about it. But it's not his concern. This is between me and Audrey. I've asked her to marry me."

A smile formed on Logan's face, and he put out his hand. "Well, congratulations."

Luke didn't make a move to shake his brother's hand. His fingers gripped the pen tighter. *Click. Click. Click.* "She turned me down."

Logan's hand dropped to his side. "Why would she do that? Anyone with eyes in their head could see she's crazy about you."

"Logan," Sophia said, her voice sweet with warning. "It's a little more complicated than that."

"How complicated can it be?" he asked.

Luke tossed the pen down. "You'd be surprised."

Without going into the intimate details, Luke painted a picture for Logan and Sophia, explaining the situation between Audrey and him. Logan could be an ass at times, but not today. Today, both he and Sophia listened and gave their support.

"Well, you gotta give her time," Logan said. "You can't blow this. There's a baby involved."

"Not too much time, though," Sophia said. She appeared thoughtful. "Women need reassurances."

"Go after what you want," Logan said. He'd been persistent with Sophia and it had paid off.

"Be genuine," Sophia said.

"Got it," Luke said. Maybe getting Audrey to agree to marry him wasn't as impossible as it seemed. Maybe he hadn't tried hard enough.

Or maybe you don't want to hurt her anymore.

Luke gave his head a quick shake. He'd been reeling from Audrey's rejection and stressed out about how to change her mind. He couldn't lie to her and tell her what she wanted to hear. That would be cruel. And she'd see right through it.

Sophia walked around the desk to give him a hug, her embrace tight with affection. Logan congratulated him about the baby if not an upcoming wedding. Luke strode out of the lodge, grateful to both for their advice. A sense of relief curled in his belly that at least his family knew the situation now. Audrey would be the mother of his child.

All day long, Luke had been thinking about her. There was something sexy and beautiful about a woman carrying your child. The notion had settled in his gut and clung there, making him smile at times, making him look at Audrey Faith Thomas differently.

Later that night, Luke sat in his bed thinking about going

after what he wanted, about being genuine and about giving Audrey reassurances. He didn't know if he could do the last thing, but two out of three wasn't bad and he had to try something.

He picked up his phone and hoped to heaven Audrey wouldn't ignore his text messages the way she had for the past few nights.

R u asleep?

Her reply came quickly.

No. I should be but I'm not tired.

Not tired, either. Keep thinking about today.

She wrote back.

Meeting the doctor and realizing we're going to be parents?

That, too. But thinking about what happened after.

Chipmunk Café?

Kissing you, Audrey.

There was a minute delay in her response.

It was a good kiss, Luke.

He had to keep her talking. He was glad she responded. Glad she hadn't shut him down.

I bought a *What To Expect When You're Going to Be a Daddy* book the other day.

R u reading it?

No, I'm texting with you. Want to read it together?

Now?

Yes.

R u really asking me to come to your room to read a baby book?

He went for broke. *Be genuine. Go after what you want.*

That would be my second choice when you got here. It's up to you, darlin'.

She was chilly from every part of her body the do-me black negligee didn't cover. That had to be why she was shivering. Any second now, things could get really hot, though. Gosh, she hoped so. Audrey squeezed her eyes shut, stood at Luke's door and knocked.

A few minutes ago, she'd nearly dropped the phone from her hands reading Luke's message. And the rebellious, wild, sadistic part of her told her to put on the skimpy black nightie, march into Luke's room and spend one last glorious night with him, reason be damned. Oddly—or maybe rightly so—she'd followed her gut instincts. Now, here she stood, trembling like a kid watching her first horror flick, her blood pulsing and her heart zipping along.

She heard footsteps approach from behind the door. Her breath caught and she choked with fear as all semblances of bravado and courage abandoned her.

The door opened to Luke, barefoot, wearing unsnapped faded jeans and nothing else.

Mercy.

The moment his eyes landed on her, they flickered and blinked and turned warm as honey as he pored over every ounce of her body. A slow, sexy smile gradually eased the corners of Luke's mouth up, making this devastatingly good-looking man even more beautiful.

How was that possible?

To think she was having a child with this man.

The notion warmed her heart.

She would love Luke until the end of time.

"I came to, to, uh—"

"Read?"

She moved her head to nod, but Luke was too fast for her. Before she could complete the gesture, he pulled her through the doorway and backed her up against the wall. He pressed his body so close she could feel the steam radiating off his broad, bare chest. "Some say reading is overrated." He cupped her shoulders, tucking his index finger underneath the spaghetti straps that held her negligee in place. He teased the straps to and fro. "I don't agree," he whispered. "You can learn a lot from the written word."

Tenderly, he slid the straps down her arms.

Her breasts popped free.

As she absorbed the impact of Luke's quick intake of breath, her eyes gently closed.

"Some books are page-turners."

He kissed her shoulders, taking little nips.

Her skin sizzled like hot oil from his touch.

"Some books you want to keep on reading."

He weighed her bosom in his hands at the same time as his mouth covered hers. A groan of pleasure and satisfaction rose from his throat and for the first time since she'd knocked on his door, she was certain she'd made the right decision coming to him tonight.

He looped her arms around his neck and continued to kiss her, giving her the sliver of heaven she'd needed tonight.

"You're beautiful, Audrey Faith."

"So are you," she whispered.

The room was cast in shades of light and dark. The silence

of the empty house surrounded them. She loved him with all her heart. He didn't love her back. She wished he would. She wished it wasn't lust but love spurring his desire for her.

"I don't know what I am doing here," she breathed through tenderly bruised lips.

Luke didn't offer platitudes but seemed to speak straight from his heart. "I'm just glad you decided to come, sweetheart."

It was enough for her. For now.

He picked her up and carried her to his bed. Laying her down carefully, he peered at her with an expression of tenderness and began to peel her nightie off. His fingers were gentle on her skin as he pulled the garment past her waist and down the legs. "I like this."

She didn't say he could thank Sophia for the do-me outfit. She only smiled.

He set the nightie at the foot of the bed and then lowered down next to her. "The doctor said lovemaking won't hurt the baby."

Audrey gave a nod. At the doctor's office, she'd blushed down to her toes when she'd heard that comment.

"I want you, Audrey." He cradled her face in his hands and kissed her again. There would be no guilt and repercussions on Luke's part. He couldn't claim foul or use his code of honor to back away. He'd invited her here tonight.

"In case you didn't notice, Luke, I'm naked on your bed. That's got to tell you something."

He chuckled and covered her with his body.

It felt right. It felt so very good.

Making love to Luke was better than ever.

And afterward as they lay together, arms and legs entwined, Luke kissed her good-night and she sighed inwardly, wishing Luke had whispered in her ear, "Some books you never want to end."

Ten

Audrey woke to an empty bed. Well, not entirely empty. She glanced to her side and picked up a lavender shoot with light purple buds lying across the sheets. She brought the pretty flower to her nose. The scent was fragrant and sweet and flavored the air in Luke's bedroom. Then she lifted the note he'd left beneath the stalk and read it silently.

Sorry to leave you. I have an early appointment in Carson City. See you tonight at dinner.
Luke

"You've got a date," she breathed softly. Pain squeezed her heart. She wished he'd declared his love for her and asked her out on a real date. Last night, she'd ignored her internal warnings to stay clear of him, to protect herself at all costs. And today, she'd pay the price for her one night of indulgence. Nothing had changed.

She rose, her bare feet hitting the hardwood floor from

the tall four-poster bed. On impulse, she turned to run her hand along the smooth Egyptian cotton sheets where Luke had made love to her. A sigh of longing escaped her throat. His hot kisses, his sensual caresses and their joined bodies totally in sync with each other meshed in her mind. She savored the heady memory.

The rest of the morning flew by. At the barn, she saddled up three horses and led each one of them up into the hilly country for long, brisk walks. Then she took time to wash down and groom each one. Audrey was in her element among the animals and the ranch hands. Today, especially, was a productive day.

Ward Halliday approached her as she was putting away tack. "Hey, Audrey."

"Good afternoon, Ward. How're you doing today?"

She turned to face him across the length of the tack room. The friendly smile that brightened his leathery face was gone. The usual spark in his eyes was gone, too. "I'm doing fine."

"Really? Because you're looking a little frazzled around the collar."

He shrugged a shoulder, his lips tight with regret. "My boy has to leave for college a week early. They moved up orientation and it's no point him going all the way to Texas and back. He's gonna stay put once he gets there."

"Oh, no! When's he leaving?"

"On the red-eye tonight. My wife, Molly, is fixing him a big farewell supper, all his favorites."

"So what are you doing here?"

"Well, I'm working. Gonna finish out the day."

She began shaking her head. There was no way Ward was going to miss being with Hunter on his last day home. "Ward, please let me finish up the few chores that are left. You should go home and be with your family. The boys can help me with anything else that needs doing."

"I appreciate that but—"

"Please, let me do this for you. Go home and spend time with Hunter today. He's probably excited and nervous and can use you around to settle him down."

Ward lifted the rim of his hat and gave her a sheepish look. "Who's gonna settle me down?"

"Molly."

Ward chuckled.

"I've got this, really. I'll make sure the horses are fed and stabled for the night."

He looked at her like a child opening an early Christmas present. "Thank you, Audrey. I'll be sure to stop by the house on our way to the airport so Hunter can say a proper good-bye to you all."

"Darn right you will. I've gotta give Hunter a big hug and some tips on college life."

Audrey walked with Ward arm in arm outside the barn doors. She watched him get into his truck, start the engine and drive along the road that led to the main highway.

Jewel brushed against her legs and she glanced down at her cat, who had pretty much taken over the Slade house perimeter. "What are you up to, Jewel?"

Meow.

"Same as usual, I see."

Audrey finished up her chores and then strode over to the other barn to see Trib. It was her daily outing, and she was thrilled to see the horse really beginning to relate to her. He no longer shied away when she opened the half door of the paddock and Jewel jumped up. The horse was turning the corner in the trust department and Audrey couldn't be more pleased.

Jewel took her seat on the ledge of the half door and looked for her new friend. Then the cat meowed and glanced at Audrey curiously. Audrey scanned the paddock. Tribute wasn't in his stall.

In her haste to convince Ward to head home, she'd forgotten about Trib and apparently so had the foreman. Now, as she walked outside and peeked around the corner of the barn, she saw Trib standing on the far end of the corral, blending into the shadows under an oak tree.

"There you are," she said congenially.

Trib spotted her and snorted. He could make this hard for her, or he could make this easy. "Come here, boy," she called to him. "Gotta get you settled for the night."

The horse gave her a stubborn stare and didn't budge. "Are you kidding me," she muttered under her breath. Apparently Trib was going to live up to his nickname of Tribulation today.

Jewel's nose nudged her leg. "Would you look at our friend over there," she said to her cat. "I think he wants me to come get him."

The horse whinnied softly and took a few steps forward, toward them. Audrey smiled. "He does. He's telling me to come get him."

Audrey knew he was ready. He was giving her his trust. Over the past few days, she'd made incredible progress with him. She had to thank Jewel for some of that; the two had become cautious, but endearing friends.

She didn't waste another second. This was an opportunity to really earn her keep around here. She was being paid to do a job, and with Ward gone, and no one else close enough to the stallion to bring him in, she knew she could do it.

Trib would cooperate.

She felt it in her bones.

The horse took another step closer, then stopped and watched her. "I'll be right there, I'm coming to get you, Trib."

She quickly walked into the barn, grabbed a handful of sugar cubes and gathered up a bridle and lead rope.

Jewel seemed bored with it all and began swatting at flies buzzing around the feed bags in the barn. Audrey left her there and walked back outside.

Taking measured steps, she kept her eyes on the horse as

she made her approach with the rope and halter in one hand and a fistful of sugar in the other.

Now out in broad sunlight, away from the dark and light shadows Trib appeared friendly and amiable. She walked within a few feet of him and put out her hand. "Here you go, boy."

He craned his neck forward and brought his mouth to her hand, nibbling away at the sugar until it was all gone.

"I've got to get you home," she said softly. Steadily, she fit the rope halter over his head and adjusted it under his chin. Trib stood still and allowed her to fasten the five-foot lead rope to the harness.

She gave his mane a soft pat. "Okay, we're almost ready. You're doing fine."

With great care, she led him forward toward the barn, all the while talking quietly and calmly to him.

Midway to the barn, she caught a glimpse of a cowboy at the fence post.

Uh-oh.

"Audrey. What in hell are you doing?" Luke spoke quietly enough not to spook the horse. But his angry tone was unmistakable.

Refusing to be distracted, she stared at the horse. "I've been working with Trib and he's ready."

"Audrey, get out of there, *right now,*" he rasped with menace in his voice.

"You're paying me to do a job." Eyes still trained on Trib, she spoke softly. "And we're doing just fine."

"You're fired. I don't want you to—"

And suddenly, out of nowhere, an orange blur appeared, racing at top speed toward her, Blackie, the Slades' Border collie, chasing Jewel and barking like crazy. Luke cursed. He bounded over the corral fence just as Trib jerked his head back and yanked on the lead rope. Audrey held on tight, as long as she could. But Trib was more powerful. The rope jerked free of her hands. She stumbled forward and managed at the last second to turn her body. She landed with a thud on her butt.

Jewel whizzed by with Blackie at her heels. It all happened so fast. Trib whinnied loudly enough for the next county to hear. He reared up, his front legs coming eight feet off the ground. Audrey froze. Seconds ticked by in slow motion as she watched the horse balance himself on his hind legs as if trying to keep from crashing down on her.

"Watch out!" Luke shouted, running toward her.

He fell to his knees and pressed her close, cosseting her with his body and creating a shield of protection around her. She thought for a split second everything would be okay.

And then the force of Trib's frustration landed on Luke with a crushing sound.

She felt a thump.

Luke bellowed in pain. And then slumped over her like a rag doll, lifeless and limp.

"Luke! Luke!"

"Don't move him!" one of the ranch hands shouted from a distance.

"We're calling for help," another one said.

Audrey held her breath, bearing Luke's weight and sending up prayers for his life.

Audrey's tears stained her shirt as she unpacked her bags with Jewel looking on. They were home. Finally back in Reno. Finally back where she belonged.

She hated herself, hated the pain and anguish she'd caused Luke. She couldn't stay on at the ranch, though everyone tried like crazy to convince her not to go. How on earth could she stay? How could she face Luke after what had happened? She had a hard enough time facing herself in the mirror.

She'd almost caused his death.

She hadn't listened to his warnings.

She wanted so badly to prove to Luke he'd been wrong about Trib.

But she was the one who'd been wrong about everything.

More tears spilled from her eyes. It wasn't good for the baby for her to cry like this, so she forced herself to stop. It was hard and she didn't deserve to give herself a break. She didn't deserve much of anything right now.

Poor Jewel. Even her cat knew something was off. Jewel glanced around her surroundings with dismay. Her sheepskin kitty bed and three-tier cat house seemed to have lost their appeal. Jewel moped. The cat had gotten accustomed to being on Slade land. She'd grown out of her separation anxiety. Living at the ranch had been like therapy.

Audrey steadied her breathing. She couldn't seem to keep a dry face. She had the feeling she would have cried just as hard even if she weren't pregnant. No, her tears couldn't be blamed on hormones. Her tears would've been shed regardless.

Inside, she bled for the big mess she'd made of things, but she couldn't think about that at the moment. She couldn't wallow in self-pity. Luke was the important one. He would survive. Though he'd be spending the next week in the hospital, he would make a full recovery.

He'd been lucky, the doctor said. The horse hooves hadn't made a direct hit. The thick-lined leather jacket Luke was wearing had lessened the impact of the force. But one hoof had knocked into the back of his head.

Luke had gotten another concussion.

Strike one for Audrey.

His body took a hard pounding.

Strike two for Audrey.

His spine wasn't injured, but all of his organs were badly bruised.

Three strikes and you're out.

As soon as she'd gotten the news that Luke would make a full recovery, she'd left the ranch. It hadn't been easy to leave, but guilt and remorse had a way of convincing her that she wasn't worthy. That sticking around would just make matters worse. She'd already caused Luke a world of grief and pain. She would've been the last person he'd want to see when he woke up in the hospital. At some point, she would have to face him, because of the baby. He'd want to know the baby was all right. She wouldn't deny him anything regarding their child, but she also didn't want to burden his life with her presence. He had every right to blame her for all the trouble she'd caused him.

Oh, he probably would never forgive her.

She couldn't fault him that; she'd never forgive herself.

Fresh tears burned behind her eyes. She squeezed them shut to prevent another flood. She would be eternally thankful to Luke for protecting the new life thriving inside her belly. The baby wasn't injured. If Luke hadn't come along when he did, who knows what would have happened?

A chill ran up and down her arms.

Our baby is safe. Thank you, Luke.

The phone rang. Audrey walked over to look at the digital number blinking on the screen.

Casey.

Like a mother hen, her brother had been calling her every day since he'd found out about the baby. Audrey didn't pick up. She let the machine get it.

"If you're there, please pick up. I need to talk to you."

Please?

Since when did her brother say please?

Audrey plucked a tissue from the box and wiped her eyes. She took another one to blow her nose. Then before the machine clicked off, she grabbed the phone.

"Hello."

"Well, you sound like death warmed over," he said.

"I love you, too."

Casey's voice was full of concern. "How are you doing, sis?"

"At the moment, I'm not putting anyone's life at risk, so I suppose it's a good day."

Her brother took an exasperated breath. "Audrey Faith."

"I'm sorry, Case. But Luke was almost killed by that horse."

"I'm gonna go out on a limb here and tell you it wasn't your fault. None of it. The horse was spooked by the confusion in the corral. If he hadn't been so darn isolated all that time, he wouldn't have gotten jittery about seeing a dog chase a cat."

"So now it's Luke's fault for keeping the horse in the paddock after he nearly trampled him the first time?"

"I'm saying it's no one's fault. It was a freakish accident."

"Luke warned me about him, Casey. And I didn't listen. I just went right ahead and did what I pleased. My gosh. Do you realize what might have happened?"

She shuddered in fear and wrapped her arm around her middle where the smallest baby bump had appeared just this week.

She was grateful to Luke for his fathering instincts. He'd rushed over to protect their child.

"And you pay him back for saving you and the baby by running out on him?"

"He fired me."

Casey sighed. "To get you outta that corral safely."

"I will work something out with Luke later on about the baby. He knows I won't keep the baby from him. He knows—"

"You won't marry him. That's what he knows."

"He doesn't love me, Casey. What kind of marriage would it be?"

If he had loved her, he would've said something to her on their last night together. He would've known by then, wouldn't he? But it wasn't in Luke to lie to get what he wanted. He was too honest. Too good a man to do that. And sadly, Audrey had to face the reality that her child wouldn't have an ideal life. He wouldn't live in a home where his parents loved each other and harmony abounded. More than likely, their child would be shuffled back and forth between two homes.

"You should go back. Luke deserves better than this," her brother said. "You both do."

"You're saying that *now?* You wanted to knock Luke on his ass the last I heard."

"He has been knocked on his ass. And you leaving when you did was like kicking him when he was down."

Her heart squeezed tight and she whispered, "That's a low blow, Casey."

"It's the truth, honey."

Audrey paused for a second. Had she made a mistake in leaving the ranch so abruptly? Casey sure thought so. She glanced at the languid cat sleeping on the bed. Jewel thought so, too. She was depressed. "The truth is, he's glad to get rid of me. I caused him nothing but trouble."

Casey cursed under his breath. "You're being stubborn."

"I take after you."

"Think about what I'm telling you. Go back to Sunset Ranch."

Audrey couldn't face Luke. Her guilt was a tangible thing that dragged her down and made her ache inside. She couldn't bear to see him hurt, bandaged up and immobile, knowing she was the cause of his agony. If that made her a coward, so be it. In her heart she knew she was saving Luke in her own way. With her gone, he could recover with no reminders of Casey's troublemaking little sister.

"Casey, I…can't. I just can't."

Luke was determined to get out of bed and have dinner tonight in the dining room. Logan and Sophia were coming and Ellie had prepared his favorite meal. Not that he had much of an appetite lately, but after five days in the hospital and three days in his own bed, it was time to get a move on. Since he'd come home, he'd refused to take pain meds other than simple ibuprofen for his lingering aches and pains. Every day he saw improvement in his mobility.

At least nothing was broken this time. His breathing was normal and his head no longer ached. As for his pride—now, that had suffered the greatest injury.

Not only had Audrey run out on him that night in the cabin, but she'd deceived him and disobeyed his instructions about Trib. Then the woman up and ran out on him again. Emptiness stole through his body and it befuddled him why anger wasn't the strongest emotion he felt.

Luke sat on the bed and took his time putting his legs into his jeans, one foot then the other. He moved slowly, testing his muscles as he bent to pull up his pants.

Okay. That wasn't so bad.

He zipped his jeans and then carefully slid his arms into a light-gray-and-black-plaid shirt. The snaps were easy. Then he frowned when he glanced at his boots. Pulling them on would be a chore, so he opted to go downstairs barefoot.

He walked down the hallway to where a batch of bright sunflowers wrapped in raffia sat in a vase on the foyer table. The card read, "I'm so sorry. Love, Audrey."

She'd sent them to him the day after he'd been hospitalized. He thought they'd die long before this and he wouldn't have the reminder every day of how badly things had spiraled out of control between them. But they'd survived and looked as if they had no intention of wilting anytime soon.

Luke felt much the same way.

"There he is," Logan said, glancing up once Luke walked into the dining room.

He and Sophia walked over to him. Sophia gave him a kiss on the cheek. Logan patted his back once as if he was afraid of injuring him.

"Sorry if I'm late," he said.

"Right on time," Logan said.

"You're looking good, Luke." Sophia smiled.

At least Luke didn't feel like a pile of crap anymore, so progress was being made.

"Ellie's in the kitchen fixing all your favorites."

Luke raised his brows. "Smells delicious. Pot roast with all the fixin's?"

His brother nodded. "That's right." The two took their seats at the table while Luke leaned against the wall and glanced out a tall window that overlooked Sunset Ranch. "It feels good to be up and dressed and walking on my own power."

"It's great to see you that way, bro."

Luke stared out the window for a few more seconds then gingerly took a seat. "You have that talk with Ward?" he asked Logan. Ward had felt guilty about Luke's injury, thinking it was his fault for abandoning his duties and leaving early that day. Two days ago, he'd offered Luke his resignation.

"Yep, we talked. Between you and me, I think we got him convinced he wasn't at fault. Can't imagine a day when I'd accept his resignation, and I told him so. I'm still waiting on your decision about Trib. I can unload him for a song, anytime you say."

Luke pursed his lips and contemplated. He didn't know if he wanted to unload the stallion right now. He was trouble, but the stallion had come a long way. And there was something about that horse that clung on and wouldn't let go.

"He's a menace," Logan said firmly.

"I can't argue with that. But Audrey's work with him did pay off." He hated to admit that, but it was true. And that day, as much as he'd wanted Audrey out of that corral and away from that horse, he'd been impressed to see the horse respond to her. To see how far Trib had come in the short time she'd been working with him. For all the trouble the horse caused him, he shouldn't blink an eye in getting rid of him. Yet he couldn't quite do it.

"Are you thinking about keeping him?" Sophia asked.

Logan gave him a dubious look. "That damn animal put you in the hospital *twice*."

Luke nodded. "I know. I know. But I've got more important things on my mind right now. Are you forgetting I've got a baby on the way?"

Sophia's voice was sympathetic. "Have you spoken with Audrey?"

Luke didn't know if he wanted to delve too far into the subject. Audrey had been on his mind a lot lately. "No, just Casey. He tells me she's doing fine."

Sophia sipped from a glass of sparkling water. "You know, when we were at the hospital waiting for you to wake up from your concussion, you kept calling out her name."

"Did I?"

Luke remembered waking up in a daze and how the first words out of his mouth were for Audrey. He'd asked the doctor if she was injured. He remembered the relief he felt to find out she wasn't harmed. Funny thing, at the time and with his mind so foggy from being knocked unconscious, he hadn't remembered about the baby. All of his concern had been for Audrey.

Logan and Sophia peered at each other and then nodded at him. "You must've asked for her a dozen times," Logan informed him.

"Once Audrey found out you were going to make a full recovery, she excused herself and walked out of the hospital," Sophia said quietly. "She was beside herself, Luke. I've never seen someone cry so hard. She feels responsible and so terrible about this. She really cares for you."

Luke took a sip of water and swallowed hard. He couldn't figure out why he wasn't angrier with her. She'd gone against his wishes deliberately and endangered herself. All he wanted now was to see her. To make sure she was all right. But she'd taken off again.

"An injured man doesn't have a woman's name on his lips for no reason," Logan said.

His brother had a point.

"Here you go, Luke," Ellie said, coming in with a large platter of pot roast, carrots and potatoes. The savory scent whetted his waning appetite. "I hope this makes you feel better." She set the dish down in the center of the table.

"Looks delicious, Ellie. I'll do my best at putting this away."

The elderly woman gave him an affectionate pat on the shoulder. "You just eat what you can. Build your strength. The biscuits and gravy are coming."

"I'll get them," Logan said. "Luke, you go on and dig in."

Logan got up to help Ellie, and Luke filled his plate. It pleased Ellie to see him take that much food, and she walked out of the room with a satisfied expression on her face.

Luke forced smiles and conversed with his family during the meal, grateful to them for being here, for worrying over him. Yet he was struck with a bitter sense of loss. Now that he was beginning to recover, he realized something was terribly wrong. And he knew exactly what that was.

That night, Luke sat up in his bed, picked up his iPhone and sent a text message to the one person who could make him feel better.

How r u?

Audrey's reply came immediately.

I'm fine. How r u?

Doing ok. How's the baby?

Healthy. I have a little bump now.

Luke choked up. He wished to heaven he could see her swell with his child.

What r u doing?

Getting ready for bed.

Luke smiled and a wave of warmth roared through his body.

What r u wearing?

The question was audacious and he knew he was playing with fire

Luke? Is your head right? R u feeling okay?

Answer my question and I'll feel a whole lot better.

Anything to make you feel better. Just my old T-shirt.

The one that says, Cowgirls Do it With Their Boots On?

Yes.

R u wearing boots now?

Of course not. I'm going to bed. Luke, I'm so, so sorry.

Apology accepted.

So, u r not mad at me?

He wouldn't lie.

Pissed beyond belief.

There was a long pause.

What can I do? I feel awful about it.

Put your boots on. The tan ones that ride up to your knees.

Why?

R u really asking why?

Another long pause.

Ok, they're on. Now what?

He missed her like crazy. She loved him and he'd thrown that love back in her face.

Now, I'm gonna imagine u on my bed, curled up next to me, boots and all. Sleep tight, sweetheart.

Luke clicked off his phone.

He lay back against his pillow and shut off the light. Closing his eyes, he imagined Audrey beside him on the bed, beside him on the ranch, beside him as they raised their children together. He imagined Audrey Faith Thomas in his life forever.

Something had always been wrong in his past relationships with women. He'd never let himself get too close. He'd never allowed himself to create a bond. The pieces of the puzzle never quite fit right.

Now he knew what was missing.

Her.

Audrey had been missing in his life.

He loved her.

The emotion knocked him upside the head and spiraled down his body, touching every ounce of his being, absorbing into his bones. He'd always had affection for Audrey, but the intense sense of loss and emptiness without her was keen and sharp. That part surprised him most. What he felt for her was real. It wasn't anything he wanted to run from. With or without a baby, he wanted a future with Audrey. Up until now, true love had been absent in his life and now he welcomed it with an open heart.

The best healing happened during the wee hours of the night when the body and soul were at rest. Luke knew that for fact now. He slept his best sleep ever, finally at peace with his emotions.

And along with the healing, came great clarity.

"Jewel, please get off Susanna's couch," Audrey said, staring her feline down. Jewel felt entitled and refused to budge off the arm of the outdated flower-print sofa. She lay there with a blank look on her face, but Audrey knew the real reason for Jewel's disobedience.

"It's okay, Audrey," Susanna said. "She won't do it any harm. It's hanging on by a thread. I'm almost ashamed to have you sitting on it."

"Don't be silly. The couch has at least another good year left in it."

"Bite your tongue."

Audrey smiled. "I have fond memories of sitting around this room with your family, Suse. The couch is part of that." Whenever there was an important event at school, or a test Audrey couldn't miss, the Harts would invite her to stay overnight. Sometimes she'd stayed for an entire weekend while Casey was gone. "Jewel's separation anxiety came back when we returned home. She won't leave my side now. I think she's punishing me for taking her away from Sunset Ranch. She loved it there."

"I think you did, too," Susanna said.

"I did, Suse, but I couldn't stay. Now with the baby coming and all, I'm going to have to make some tough decisions. I have to postpone veterinarian school for another year. Dr. Arroyo offered me a full-time job in the vet clinic. It means long hours, but doing something I love to do."

"And your hunky Luke's okay with the whole situation?"

Audrey wished he *was* her hunky Luke. Unshielded guilt consumed her. She'd been nothing but trouble for Lucas Slade. Still, she looked forward to the nightly text messages she'd been getting from him lately. They made her whole day worthwhile. She found herself anxiously awaiting the evening hours to hear from him. But it was Luke being Luke. Checking up on her. Making sure the baby was okay. She was certain any day now he'd bring up the subject of custody. How would they work out the details?

"It's early yet. I'm only nine weeks along. I think we're just getting used to the idea of becoming parents so we haven't discussed it yet. But…but I'm sure we will. Luke wants to be a big part of the baby's life."

Just not a part of hers.

He offered to marry you and you turned him down.

"I hope you have a good time at Casey's tomorrow," Susanna said. "I'm glad you decided to visit him. Maybe being at the lake will help clear your mind."

She hoped a trip to the cabin would help her get a handle on her chaotic emotions. There were too many variables in her life now—joy about the baby but heartache over Luke. She had indecision about the job offer and worried about what her future would hold. All of it made her queasy with anxiety.

"I hope so, too. So long as Casey doesn't dwell on my pitiful life, I think I'll be fine. My brother is convinced he knows what's best for me."

Susanna smiled. "Casey misses you. I think you'll have a good time together."

"You're right. Gosh, I'm sorry I'm such a downer lately."

"Hey, you've been there for me, too. That's what friends are for."

They said good-night with an embrace and Audrey went home to pack a few things.

In the morning, she made the drive to the north shore of Lake Tahoe with Jewel beside her in the travel carrier. Fall was beginning to show signs in the crispness of the air and the fresh scent of pine. Early sunlight cast the lake in shades of indigo that gleamed off the water and brightened her entire outlook.

Casey came out to greet her and they hugged tight. He was full of questions about the baby, and as they headed inside the cabin, she laughed at some of the silly notions he had in his head about pregnancy. Not that she was an expert, but she was pretty sure that no, the shape of the woman's belly did not determine the baby's sex. And yes, it was true that she would probably develop a dark hormone line that would run from the top of her torso to below her navel that would divide her body almost in half. No, she wouldn't need to drink the two half gallons of milk in his refrigerator to build up her milk supply. "Goodness, Casey. I'm only staying two days. You've got enough milk in here for an entire kindergarten class."

"Well, just making sure you have what you need."

She kissed his cheek and they spent the entire afternoon being lazy on the deck, stretched out on cushioned chaise longues and watching a few local sunbathers trying to catch the last rays of warmth for the season.

"Pretty soon, snow will top the mountains," she said.

"Not soon enough for the skiers," Casey said. "They can't wait for the cold weather to hit." He tilted his head and gave her a tentative look. "I've got reservations at Emeralds for tonight. We never had a chance to celebrate you having a baby. You up for it?"

Audrey reached over to touch his hand. "That's sweet, Casey. Yes, I'm up for it."

"No pets allowed. Think Jewel here will let you go?"

Jewel's head perked up from her prone position on the patio deck at the mention of her name.

"Knowing Jewel, after she eats she'll probably pass out in front of the fireplace. She won't know I'm gone."

Casey gave her a nod of approval. "Smart cat."

Audrey chuckled. "Thanks, Casey for…well, for not being so, so…"

"I'm trying, honey. You'll always be my little sis, and I'll always watch out for you, but I get that you're all grown-up now. You don't need me anymore."

"I need you, Casey. Just not your interference in my life. I'm ready to make my own decisions," she said softly.

He swallowed and stared out at the lake.

That evening they had dinner at an exclusive restaurant with a spectacular view of Emerald Bay. The crescent-shaped alcove cradled shallow, pale emerald-green waters. Fanette Island reached out of the center of the bay with a Hershey Kiss–topped peak. The food was delicious and Audrey's mood lightened being with her brother.

By the time they returned to the cabin, Audrey was beat. "I'm going to bed," she said to Casey. "Thanks for a wonderful dinner. I'll see you in the morning." She reached up on tiptoes and gave Casey a peck on the cheek.

"Good night, Sis."

Audrey showered and dressed in an old T-shirt. Some people had comfort food, but Audrey had comfort wear. She was cozy in worn-out, old bed clothes that felt soft against her skin. The baby seemed to love it, too. She snuggled into the bed and when the ringtone barked, she picked up her phone and read the text. It was Luke.

How r u?

Fair. How r u?

Fair. But now that I'm talking to you, I'm better.

Audrey squeezed her eyes closed. A viselike grip tightened on her heart. More and more now, Luke would say something sweet like this, or make an innuendo that begged an invitation from her. She didn't have the courage to act upon it. She couldn't face another rejection. And then, there was the guilt she harbored that reminded her daily of the injuries she'd caused him.

I'm glad you're feeling better.

R u in bed?

Yes.

In a T-shirt?

Yes.

Well?

It says *Cowgirls Party in the Paddock.*

Luke didn't waste a second to answer.

Sounds like a party I'd want to attend.

Mercy. Audrey nibbled on her lower lip.

I'm not a party girl.

Could've fooled me a few months ago.

Are you still pissed?

That you seduced me then ran away? That you lied to me? That you disobeyed my orders with Trib?

Her hopes faded.

I guess I have my answer.

I'm mellowing.

Doesn't sound like it.

Do you still love me?

Audrey couldn't believe he was asking her that. A person didn't fall out of love that easily. It just showed how little Luke knew about love. And about her. She'd loved him for ten years. She couldn't just forget about that because things didn't work out. Life was messy and she'd certainly stepped in it this time. If anything, her love for him had grown stronger after he'd saved her and the baby.

It doesn't matter.

You don't love me.

I take that as a yes. There's going to be a knock at your door any second.

What? Panicked, she glanced at the bedroom door before she remembered she was at the cabin. She typed,

I'm not home.

I know.

Then the door opened and Luke strode in, cell phone in hand.

She jumped and hit her head against the backboard of the bed. "Luke!"

He tucked the phone into his pocket. "I gave you warning."

"You...you didn't knock."

"Didn't I?" He grinned and moved farther into the room. "Seems to me you didn't knock a few months back when you crept in here and destroyed my sleep."

"Wh-what are you doing here?"

This whole thing reeked of Casey *not interfering.* Her brother must've set this up.

But oh, how she'd missed Luke. His devastating smile and the light in his eyes were enough to floor any female, much less one who was already crazy about him. She tossed the covers off and was about to get out of bed when Luke's piercing gaze froze her in place. He sat down next to her. The scent of leather and musk put her mind in a tizzy.

Jewel woke from solid sleep, got up and rubbed at the back of his legs. He bent to scratch her behind the ears and she purred so loudly, it echoed off the walls. Traitorous cat. "Did Casey put you up to this? I'm going to—"

"I did some fast talking with Case to get him to allow me to come here. This was all my idea." He glanced around the room and then his reverent gaze touched on her. "This room is where our baby was conceived."

"I...I know."

Her mind was muddled. It was late. She was tired. She couldn't think straight with him sitting on her bed, so near. If he wanted to talk custody in legal terms, she couldn't do it. "I can't think right now, Luke. Can we talk another time? Maybe, if you came back in the morning."

He gave his head a shake. "You're a flight risk, Audrey. I'm not giving you a chance to take off again. Seems that's what you do to me. Leave."

"That's only because—"

"I love you, Audrey."

"Wh-what?"

"I said, I love you. I need you in my life. I'm not leaving here until I convince you of that."

The words were foreign to her ears. Luke didn't love her. How could he? She'd done horrible things to him. She'd nearly caused his death, for heaven's sake. "You love the baby."

"True. I love the baby. It's a part of you, sweetheart. That baby is the best part of both of us. If I didn't love you, why on earth would I forgive you for everything you've done? Why would I call out your name when I was unconscious? Yes, I did that, they tell me. And as soon as I woke up, your name was the first on my lips. I called for you, Audrey. And you weren't there. It was an awful feeling. It hurt more than my injuries."

"Oh, Luke. I'm so sorry about that. I hated to leave you, but I thought I'd be the last person you'd want to see when you woke up."

"You left Sunset Ranch without saying goodbye."

Her guilt was as sharp as the tip of a knife.

Luke reached for her hands. He applied gentle pressure that shot straight to her heart and made her hope for the first time in a long time. Then he looked her square in the eyes. "I've never lied to you, Audrey. I think you know that about me. I asked you to marry me, but I didn't tell you I loved you. I didn't know it then, but I know it now."

Audrey's hope register shot up. "Wh-why do you know it now?"

Luke looked past her, as if trying to find a way to explain it. "I thought I wasn't capable of love or allowing myself to get close to anyone for anything other than friendship. It has to do with my roots and my love of a horse that was taken away when I was very young. It didn't help to see the kind of marriage my folks had. I guess I put up barriers and wouldn't let anyone breach them. Until Trib came along."

"Trib? I don't understand."

"For some reason that horse got under my skin. Even after all the trials and tribulations and the trouble he caused, I can't seem to part with him. I see his spirit and know he'll be mine one day. I don't ever intend on letting him go. Now don't take this the wrong way, but that's exactly how I feel about you. You and Trib have a lot in common."

Audrey's brows knitted together as she tried to make sense of it.

Luke continued, "I never let myself get close to any of the animals on the ranch after that one devastating incident when I was a boy. It scarred me for life. So I steered clear and when I felt like I was feeling more than I should, I would back off and detach myself for fear of being hurt. Just recently, I realized I did that very same thing with women. Until you came back into my life. That's how I know I love you. After all the deception and lies you told, Audrey, I couldn't dismiss you. I wouldn't even consider firing you."

"You did fire me."

"That was bogus. I was desperate to get you away from Trib. I was falling in love with you and didn't realize it."

Audrey's heart was ready to burst. Still, she droned, "Because I reminded you of a horse?"

His eyes grew serious, as if this next question meant a great deal. "But you get it, right?"

His honest plea had her convinced. She nodded. "I think so."

He continued, "I told myself I had a physical attraction to you and I'd get over it. But I didn't get over it. I couldn't write you off like I had all the others. Because as much trouble as you've caused me, I didn't give up on you. I didn't back off. Then when I learned you were pregnant, I wanted to marry you because it was the right thing to do. And you were right to refuse me. I see that now. When I lay hurt in that hospital bed, I began to see my future without you. And it was a killer. I never want to feel that way again. I don't want to live my life without you, Audrey. To me, you're perfect just the way you are."

"Oh, Luke." Tears welled in her eyes.

He smiled and kissed her fingertips. "You're amazing and talented and smart. You're pretty and sexy and you make me laugh. This isn't about the baby, Audrey. I swear, I really do love you."

Audrey's hope soared. Luke never lied. He would stretch the truth at times to keep his dashing knight status, but he never flat-out lied. "I love you, too."

Luke grinned. "Thank God. I was worried."

He was worrying about her love for him? Not a chance in hell that would ever change. But she did have one tidbit that she needed to come clean about. She held her breath, vowing to strive to be Miss Goody Two-shoes, if only he could forgive her this one last thing. "I, uh, I do have to fill you in on something that might make you angry."

Luke squinted as if he was afraid to hear what she had to say. "Lay it on me."

"It's not really a lie, exactly, just an omission of truth. When you were being so bullheaded about Trib, I sort of went behind your back to work with him late at night. After you went to bed."

Luke ground his teeth together and she could tell how hard he was trying to keep his cool, but the vein popping out of his neck was a dead giveaway. "So you're saying after I fell asleep, you'd head out to the barn in secret?"

"Yes, with Jewel. Trib took a shine to the cat and it helped me make a breakthrough."

He was silent for thirty seconds.

"Are you angry?" she finally squeaked.

"That depends on whether you'll marry me or not?"

"That's a heck of a proposal, Luke."

"Don't push it, sweetheart. I'm envisioning all the things that could've happened to you out there. And it's not sending endorphins racing through my body."

Shoot, she hoped she hadn't just ruined the moment.

She thought back to the time when she was sixteen and Luke had come to her rescue with those two boys. He'd made her a deal and asked one thing of her. Audrey would honor that vow now. She put her heart on the line and gave him her answer. "I promise you, Lucas Slade, I won't do anything reckless or dangerous after we're married."

"So you'll marry me?" A smile spread across his face, and he seemed to forget about her confession.

Audrey couldn't hide her relief. Her words rushed out, "Yes, of course I'll marry you, Luke." She looped her arms around his neck. "I love you with all of my heart. Our baby thinks he's getting a pretty good dad, too."

Luke put his hand over her belly and felt the little bump developing. The blue in his eyes deepened with love. "We're going to be a great family."

"I think so, too," Audrey said. Her dreams, her fantasies were all coming true. She was over-the-moon happy.

Luke brought his lips to hers and took her in a lingering kiss that knocked out any iota of doubt she had about his love for her.

"I missed you," he said, drawing her up tight, his gaze scorching right through her T-shirt. "I want to party with my cowgirl."

"Oh, I want that, too, but Casey—"

"Is gone. I told him he'd better get out of Dodge if he wanted me to make a legitimate woman out of you."

Audrey's laugh came out throaty and pure, her heart filled with joy.

Luke laid her down on the bed and spread his body next to hers. She shuddered in anticipation.

"I owe you a seduction," he rasped. "Payback is usually a bitch, but this time, I'm going to make sure it takes us straight to heaven. Hang on to the bedpost, sweetheart. We're going for a long, sweet ride."

Audrey closed her eyes.

She hung on.

She loved Lucas Slade inside and out.

And her knight in shining armor, Mr. Nice Guy and Good Samaritan all rolled up into one, gave her a night she would remember for all their sunsets to come.

* * * * *

COMING NEXT MONTH from Harlequin Desire®
AVAILABLE JULY 1, 2013

#2239 ZANE
The Westmorelands
Brenda Jackson
No woman walks away from Zane Westmoreland! But when Channing Hastings does just that, the rancher vows to prove to her that there is no man for her but him.

#2240 RUMOR HAS IT
Texas Cattleman's Club: The Missing Mogul
Maureen Child
Hurtful gossip once tore Sheriff Nathan Battle and Amanda Altman apart. But when Amanda comes home, will an unexpected pregnancy drive a new wedge between them or finally heal old wounds?

#2241 THE SANTANA HEIR
Billionaires and Babies
Elizabeth Lane
Grace wants to adopt her late sister's son. Peruvian bachelor Emilio wants his brother's heir...and Grace in his bed. Can this bargaining-chip baby make them a *real* family?

#2242 A BABY BETWEEN FRIENDS
The Good, the Bad and the Texan
Kathie DeNosky
Wary of men but wanting a baby, Summer asks her best friend, rancher and bullfighter Ryder, to help her conceive. But can he share his bed with her without also sharing his heart?

#2243 TEMPTATION ON HIS TERMS
The Hunter Pact
Robyn Grady
Movie producer Dex Hunter needs a nanny, and Shelby Scott is perfect for the role. But when the script switches to romance, Shelby balks at the Hollywood happy ending, at least at first....

#2244 ONE NIGHT WITH THE SHEIKH
Kristi Gold
Recently widowed King Mehdi turns to former flame Maysa Barad for solace. But as forbidden desire resurfaces, betrayal and secrets threaten to destroy their relationship once and for all.

You can find more information on upcoming Harlequin® titles, free excerpts and more at www.Harlequin.com.

HDCNM0613

REQUEST YOUR FREE BOOKS!
2 FREE NOVELS PLUS 2 FREE GIFTS!

HARLEQUIN®

Desire

ALWAYS POWERFUL, PASSIONATE AND PROVOCATIVE

YES! Please send me 2 FREE Harlequin Desire® novels and my 2 FREE gifts (gifts are worth about $10). After receiving them, if I don't wish to receive any more books, I can return the shipping statement marked "cancel." If I don't cancel, I will receive 6 brand-new novels every month and be billed just $4.55 per book in the U.S. or $4.99 per book in Canada. That's a savings of at least 13% off the cover price! It's quite a bargain! Shipping and handling is just 50¢ per book in the U.S. and 75¢ per book in Canada.* I understand that accepting the 2 free books and gifts places me under no obligation to buy anything. I can always return a shipment and cancel at any time. Even if I never buy another book, the two free books and gifts are mine to keep forever.

225/326 HDN F4ZC

Name _____ (PLEASE PRINT) _____

Address _____ Apt. # _____

City _____ State/Prov. _____ Zip/Postal Code _____

Signature (if under 18, a parent or guardian must sign)

Mail to the Harlequin® Reader Service:
IN U.S.A.: P.O. Box 1867, Buffalo, NY 14240-1867
IN CANADA: P.O. Box 609, Fort Erie, Ontario L2A 5X3

Want to try two free books from another line?
Call 1-800-873-8635 or visit www.ReaderService.com.

* Terms and prices subject to change without notice. Prices do not include applicable taxes. Sales tax applicable in N.Y. Canadian residents will be charged applicable taxes. Offer not valid in Quebec. This offer is limited to one order per household. Not valid for current subscribers to Harlequin Desire books. All orders subject to credit approval. Credit or debit balances in a customer's account(s) may be offset by any other outstanding balance owed by or to the customer. Please allow 4 to 6 weeks for delivery. Offer available while quantities last.

Your Privacy—The Harlequin® Reader Service is committed to protecting your privacy. Our Privacy Policy is available online at www.ReaderService.com or upon request from the Harlequin Reader Service.

We make a portion of our mailing list available to reputable third parties that offer products we believe may interest you. If you prefer that we not exchange your name with third parties, or if you wish to clarify or modify your communication preferences, please visit us at www.ReaderService.com/consumerchoice or write to us at Harlequin Reader Service Preference Service, P.O. Box 9062, Buffalo, NY 14269. Include your complete name and address.

HD13R

SPECIAL EXCERPT FROM

HARLEQUIN

Desire

USA TODAY *bestselling author*

Kathie DeNosky presents

A BABY BETWEEN FRIENDS, *part of the series*

THE GOOD, THE BAD AND THE TEXAN.

Available July 2013 from Harlequin® Desire®!

They fell into a comfortable silence while Ryder drove through the star-studded Texas night.

Her best friend was the real deal—honest, intelligent, easygoing and loyal to a fault. And it was only recently that she'd allowed herself to notice how incredibly good-looking he was. That was one reason she'd purposely waited until they were alone in his truck where it was dark so she wouldn't have to meet his gaze.

The time had come to start the conversation that would either help her dream come true—or send her in search of someone else to assist her.

"I've been doing a lot of thinking lately…" she began. "I miss being part of a family."

"I know, darlin'." He reached across the console to cover her hand with his. "But one day you'll find someone and settle down, and then you'll not only be part of his family, you can start one of your own."

"That's not going to happen," she said, shaking her head. "I have absolutely no interest in getting married. These days it's quite common for a woman to choose single motherhood."

"Well, there are a lot of kids who need a good home," he concurred, his tone filled with understanding.

"I'm not talking about adopting," Summer said, "at least not yet. I'd like to experience all aspects of motherhood, if I can, and that includes being pregnant."

"The last I heard, being pregnant is kind of difficult without the benefit of a man being involved," he said with a wry smile.

"Yes, to a certain degree, a man would need to be involved."

"Oh, so you're going to visit a sperm bank?" He didn't sound judgmental and she took that as a positive sign.

"No." She shook her head. "I'd rather know my baby's father."

Ryder looked confused. "Then how do you figure on making this happen if you're unwilling to wait until you meet someone and you don't want to visit a sperm bank?"

Her pulse sped up. "I have a donor in mind."

"Well, I guess if the guy's agreeable that would work," he said thoughtfully. "Anybody I know?"

"Yes." She paused for a moment to shore up her courage. Then, before she lost her nerve, she blurted out, "I want you to be the father of my baby, Ryder."

Will Ryder say yes?

Find out in Kathie DeNosky's new novel

A BABY BETWEEN FRIENDS

Available July 2013 from Harlequin® Desire®!

Copyright © 2013 by Kathie DeNosky

ALWAYS POWERFUL, PASSIONATE AND PROVOCATIVE.

THE SANTANA HEIR

by Elizabeth Lane

Grace wants to adopt her late sister's son. Peruvian
bachelor Emilio wants his brother's heir…and he wants
Grace in his bed. Can this bargaining-chip baby make
them a *real* family?

Look for the latest book in the scandalous
Billionaires and Babies miniseries next month!

Available wherever books and ebooks are sold.

HD73254